T. TOP PUBLISHING PRESENTS

BREAKING NEWS 2

BOOK 2 OF 3

BALTIMORE'S BEST SELLING AUTHOR

KAYO

Breaking News 2

Unusual Suspects
Book 2 of 2

By Kayo

First print: 2017 Nov

This is a book of fiction. Any references or similarities to actual events, real people, or real locations, are intended to give the novel a sense of reality. Any similarity to other names, characters, places and incidents are entirely coincidental.

ISBN-13: 9781981246410

Contact Information:
T. Top Publishing
Keven Gary #43319037
Kevingary400887@gmail.com
IG: @theauthorkayo
FB: Frienemies Author Kayo

Cover Design: Dynasty's Visionary Designs (Cover Me)
Facebook: www.facebook.com/dynastys.coverme
Email: covermeservice@yahoo.com

T. TOP
PUBLISHING

DEDICATION

I want to dedicate this book to my brother who passed away behind the wall.

Sherman Pride, aka DARK BLAQUE. Homeboy you will be missed. Much Ruspect to you and your family that you left behind. 400 Gun Salute to you brother.

TTIP to all the Trojans we lost along the way:

Shottie Ru

Boosie Ru

Live Wire Ru

Redz Ru

Ivory Ru

Dutch Ru

Saho Ru

Bear Ru

Von Dutch Ru

Lady Geez Ru

And last, but certainly not FOURgotten Kapo Ru bang in peace brothers & sisters.

PART 2

PAY BACK'S A BITCH

CHAPTER 18
Kinship Connection

The swelling had subsided in his face completely. The blood clots and bruises remained, but he was looking much better. His ribs were feeling a lot better, his nose was set after the swelling went down, his wrist was healing, as well as his eyes. The teeth implant surgery that was performed by Dr. Dawn Merguerian was a success, and looked perfect on him.

Today he was leaving the hospital after being in there for a month. He was happy because he was sick of it. He gave Nurse Jones, Azarah's number and told her to call her any time. She wished him the best and walked him to the door.

Azarah was at the curb, waiting, in her Audi A8 when he came out in a hoody and dark shades. He hugged Nurse Jones and got in the car. Azarah waved and pulled off.

"Where are we going, bae?"

"I'm still thinking."

"What?"

"I haven't made up my mind up yet," he said. He had never invited no one outside of his immediate circle to his house before and he wasn't entirely sure if he wanted to invite Azarah to where he laid his head. He knew that if he did, there was no turning back.

"You want to go to my house?" she asked.

"No."

"Still don't trust me?"

"It ain't that. It's just, I won't be comfortable at your house. You feel me?"

"Whatever," she said, continuing to drive with no clear destination. She grabbed the stereo remote and cut the music on.

4Hunnid began smiling as his homeboy's voice came through the speakers. He didn't say a word for the first six songs of the Undrafted mixtape. When Illuminati came on, he rapped his verse.

"Illuminati rap nigga, watch who you drinkin' wit', watch who you smokin' wit'/2 point 7 seven in my safe when I open it, if I put seven in ya face will I open it/and I know tomorrow ain't promised, but I hope it is/love to get acquainted wit'chu, stay and tear the block up/did it for my Rus so I had to put the bails up, get them things up/so I had to pick the scales up/treat you like ah rott', get'cha ears and ya tail cut/throwing the diamond sign up, niggas like what the fuck..."

Azarah stole glances of him out the corner of her eye. "My nigga Nyse really did this shit. Undrafted is a fuckin' classic. The streets will be ready for ah album soon."

"I agree. I love the mixtape."

After an hour of driving aimlessly she was tired. "Come on bae. Can you make your mind up? I'm tired."

"Can you cook?" 4Hunnid asked.

"Of course."

"I'm not talking about boiled eggs, hotdogs, and salad."

She put her middle finger up.

"I'm serious. I'm hungry, and I want a real meal."

"I can cook."

"Is there anything you can't do?"

"As a matter fact, there is. I can't do disloyal niggas. I can't do cloppy niggas. I can't do disrespect. I can't do—"

"Okay, okay, okay. I get the point. Turn up here," he said.

They ended up in the parking lot of a Super Giants' market. He wrote out a list of stuff for her to get, and he instructed her to grab everything she would need to cook dinner every night for a month.

He pulled a thousand dollars from his pocket and handed it to her.

"Pay a few of the workers to help you get the bags in the car."

"Yes, sir," she said, smiled and got out.

He put the disc back on track number three; Grown Man Bars and laid his seat back.

"Damn Nyse, you murdered this shit."

When Azarah came out of the market 4Hunnid was parked out front with the trunk open. With help from a few Giants' workers, she packed the trunk, and the back seat with eight hundred dollars worth of groceries.

"I'm still mad at you King Tremaine Davenport," she said, when she pulled off.

"Make a right here. When you get to the light make a left."

"To the freeway?"

"Yeah," he said. "What did I do now, for you to be using my whole name?"

"About my car. You made me put tints on my windows."

"So you liked the fishbowl look?" he asked.

"Yes, I did. I didn't even know what presidential tints were, until now."

"Don't worry, Sexy. When I get four hunnid percent and come back out, you can take them off."

Thirty minutes later they were pulling down a block in Walnut Hill, Maryland with the prettiest houses Azarah had ever seen.

She was feeling how considerate he was by her fascination with the pretty houses, letting her circle the block a few times.

4Hunnid was watching everything behind the dark Balenciaga shades. He pulled an object from his jeans that resembled a flash drive.

"Pay attention Azarah."

"What?"

"Pay attention," he said. When she got three houses from the end of the block, that she came down three times already, he hit a button on the object and said, "Make a left into this driveway and pull all the way in the garage."

She did as she was told and pulled in next to a Jeep Cherokee SRT. The garage closed behind them. "Where are we?"

"Inside my domain. Welcome." He got out and began grabbing bags. It took him a few tries to find the right key.

"You okay, Bae?"

"Yeah. All my locks were changed, so I had to find the right one. I'm good though. Come on."

They had all of the bags in the kitchen in twenty minutes. He took her on a tour of his home. She wasn't surprised that his house was laid out in all the finest of everything. She found it hard to believe that he had acquired these fortunes off of two years of rapping, only, but she didn't dwell on it too long.

"So, what do you think?" he asked, with his hands in the air.

"It's beautiful. I didn't take you as the type of man with good taste." She smiled.

"I'll take that as a compliment."

"Question. Why did you have me get dog food? I didn't see a dog in here."

He didn't say anything. He just pointed behind her. She turned around and saw the meanest looking dog she ever saw. The big black dog had her sharp teeth exposed, with drool coming down both sides of her strong jaws.

"I'm scared, Bae," she said, scared to move.

He laughed.

"This is Two T's, Sexy. My twenty-six inch, hundred pound female Boxer. Two T's, meet Queen Azarah Williams aka Soulful, known to me as Sexy. My dog is very loyal to me. She does exactly what I tell her to do."

"I'll keep that in mind," she said, still scared to move.

"Close your mouth Two T's." The dog closed her mouth. "Come'eer. You missed me. Did the lawyer lady come walk and feed you like I asked her to?"

Roof! Azarah jumped at her bark.

"Good. Go to your room, you scaring Sexy."

Two T's looked at Azarah, turned her nose up at her, and walked away.

"Did she just mug me?"

"Two T's is very territorial."

"Damn, I haven't even been in here for an hour and I already have to worry about another bitch," she said, causing them both to laugh.

"Are you cooking dinner tonight?"

"I can, if you want me to."

"I do. I'm hungry as shit. I just came off that stupid-ass liquid diet from my oral surgery."

"Dawn did an excellent job on your teeth."

"She sure did," he agreed. "I'm going to get in the shower while you handle your business down here in the kitchen," he said, and clapped his hands twice.

She looked at him strange when he did it and began taking items from out the grocery bags. When she turned back around Two T's was right there watching her silently, like a hawk.

"Go somewhere, dog," she shooed, but Two T's stayed put, deathly still.

4Hunnid got in the shower and let the hot water run down on top of his dreaded head, with all types of thoughts running through his head. When he had a clouded head, he would usually go to The Dungeon and put his feelings on a track. Going to Toe Taggin' Attire was out of the question, so he'd have to settle for the studio in his basement, which was state-of-the art as well.

So many thoughts ran through his head as the water showered his battered body. He knew he had to find and kill Traum before he did anything else. Traum didn't have the money, he knew, to leave the country, so he was still in the city.

Just like you can't hide from the feds without money, you can't hide from me, he thought.

Falling back on his queen size bed in nothing but a burgundy beach towel never felt so good. The food that was being cooked downstairs was assaulting his nose. It smelled delicious.

His house phone rung, causing him to sit up immediately.

"Yo," he answered.

"How are you doing warrior?"

"Connie Y, what's up?"

"You tell me."

"I'm okay. Gettin' better. Thanks for checkin' on me."

"I have to. Your family wants answers. They all call me, all day, everyday."

"They'll be aiight. I'll be back soon."

"Okay. I'm calling because a Detective Lin contacted me about you."

"What did he say?"

"He basically wanted to know where to find you and did you remember anything else about the kidnapping or the other guy involved. I told him that you didn't remember anything else and that everything would be coming through me. He asked me did you still live on Baltimore Street. So he pulled your license. I told him you did. So they'll have someone on the house for sure."

"Thanks Lawyer Lady... for everything. You are one of ah kind."

"Your welcome 4Hunnid. You're family."

"Your words match your actions, so I'm cool with that," he said. "What's up with that other thing we spoke about?"

"It's being done now as we speak. You may be able to pick it up tomorrow."

"Okay," he said. There was an awkward silence between them afterwards. "What's on ya mind Connie?" He heard her sniffle.

"I worry about you KT."

"I know you do, but I'm good Aunt Connie."

"You better be. I love you."

"Love you more," he said and put the phone back in its cradle.

Azarah came upstairs a few minutes later. She saw him laid back in the bed with just a towel on. She said a silent prayer, thanking God for keeping him safe throughout the entire ordeal of the kidnapping.

"What'chu doing?" he asked, catching her with her eyes closed.

"Nothing."

"Nothing? Looked to me like you were praying. Is that what you were doing?"

"So, what if I was?"

"I didn't say it was a problem. Just don't say it was nothing, when it clearly was."

"You got that, King."

"Come, sit," he said, patting the space next to him.

"Fool, I am not Two T's."

"Come'eer girl and sit'cho phat-ass right here next to me."

She moved towards him quickly.

"What," she asked, sitting down.

He put his hand through her long locks of Malaycian hair. She put her hands on his bruised chest, then traced the lines of tho tattooed Tree on his chest. He put his hands up her 887 t-shirt and unhooked her bra strap. She removed the burgundy beach towel, exposing him in all his glory. He pulled her shirt up over her head, exposing her peanut butter, brown breast, dark brown areolas, and her rapidly hardening nipples.

A soft moan escaped her lips when his hands found their way to her nipples. He worked his way around her breast like he had done it a million times before. He brung his mouth down on her left breast, while he fondled the right one. She ran her hands through her dreads. Her breathing became heavy.

He stopped and she looked at him.

She stood up and removed her pants and panties. He stared at her shaved, inviting mound and licked his lips with his long tongue. He got up and pushed her on the bed. He pushed her ankles up, so that her knees were in the air, and spread her legs open. He dove head first between her legs and locked on to her privates.

"Ahhh! Shit!" she exclaimed, wrapping her hands in his hair. "Oh... my... fu... fuc... King... shit... gawd!" His tongue was so long it touched places inside of her that had never been touched before.

"I'm... shit... sh... shit... cum... cumming! Oh... lord! Shit! Ahhh!" she cried out as the orgasm took control of her shaking body.

4Hunnid got up and looked down on her beautiful body and sexy face, admiring what laid before him.

She looked up at him, in his eyes, and saw nothing but confidence and determination.

"You ready?" he asked.

"I been ready from the moment I first saw you. I just had to make sure you were."

"Oh, I'm ready."

"Why you still talking then, 4Hunnid? Come get it." He didn't have to be told twice. He got in it like she wanted him to; for an explosive twenty minutes.

Afterwards she laid in his arms, wanting to be there forever. Somehow, she felt like there was no such thing as forever with a guy like King Tremaine Davenport. "What'chu thinking about, Azarah?"

"Us."

"What about us?" he asked, fondling her breast.

"Is this real?"

"I would hope so."

"You got the pussy now. The chase is over."

"That's what'chu call gettin' the pussy? Even if that was the case, you think this is it? Yo, I never, ever, brung a female to my house. The only female to ever cross this threshold is my aunt; Connie Y. That has to count for something. My house is my safety. The only niggas that know where I live is Jerrod, Madd Lou, Magic, Trigg, and Wild Bill. And they know, but only Madd Lou been here. I don't do this. This shit is new to me. I've never been in a relationship before. I don't even know what it is really. I just know I wanna be in one with you. I'm just hoping you help ah nigga along the way."

"A relationship is trusting one another. It's communicating with one another. It's being loyal and honoring one another. It's about being honest. Are you roady for that, King?"

"I can lay here and say yeah, but only time will tell that. I don't and won't know if I'm ready, until I'm in a situation to prove myself. Shit, at one point in my life I was addicted to threesomes. It was something I loved doing. I don't know if I got it outta my system or what."

"That's not a problem; I'm bi-sexual. So long as we can set some rules. I don't have a problem with bringing a bad bitch in our bed."

4Hunnid had to smile as he thought about getting it in with Azarah and another bad chick.

"You like that, don't you?" she asked.

"I respect your authenticity, Queen."

"And I respect your gangster, King."

"What's up with the food?"

"You still hungry," she joked. "I'm joking, bae. Two T's watching it." She put her panties and t-shirt on and stood up. "Stay here until I call you."

"Yes, ma'am."

He took the opportunity to hop in the shower again, and brush his teeth. He put on his Jordan hooping shorts and Louie house shoes, and grabbed the remote to his TV. He was three minutes into the TV when he heard Azarah call his name.

The second he walked out of his room his mouth began to water from the sweet-smelling aroma from the food. "Damn girl," he said, making his way to the kitchen.

Two T's was still on guard in the same spot he left her. 4Hunnid loved his dog's discipline and loyalty. "Two T's, you smell that?"

Woof!

"Damn, you really did ya thing, ma. What is all this?"

"Fried crab cakes here. Fried Alaskan cod shrimp there. Oysters and calamari over there, and fish stew with spicy garlic rouille there."

"Sounds good, let's eat." She had finished her second fried crab cake, when she said, "I need to go past my house bae."

"What? You not comfortable?"

"Of course, I am. I just need some things from my house. Womenly things. Clothes. Underwear. Accessories. I'm almost certain you want me in the bed next to you every night while you're recovering."

"I can go for that, but you gotta do it how I say do it."

"Huh?"

"The way things are right now, we gotta take every precaution when moving around. You here in my house. I want you here, in my house. But, I wanna keep my house off the radar."

"Just let me know what you need me to do and I'll do it."

"You gotta go to work. You got ah album to put out. Whenever you come back here, it's mandatory that you make sure you're not followed. You noticed how we went around the block a few times when we got to this block? That's what I want you to do."

"I hear you bae."

"Do you, really?"

"Yes, I want us safe too."

"Okay, then keep us safe," he said.

CHAPTER 19
The Truth Shall Set You Free

Looney Redz and Samantha walked in Looney's father's house with a few bags of groceries.

"Yo Pop! We here."

His father's young girlfriend; Brandi, came bouncing down the steps in a tank top, no bra, and a pair of tight house pants that showed every curve of her forty-two inches.

Samantha hated Brandi and only tolerated her because of Looney Redz and Loon; his father. They always got into it over Brandi's flirting with her man. But Brandi didn't like her either, and didn't respect her for dealing with two brothers. So, every chance Brandi got, she made it her business to disrespect, agitate, and piss-off the half white, half black beauty.

Brandi bounced over to them with her bubbly personality and gave Looney Redz a hug, making sure to smash her size 40 H breasts up against him. He never got tired of them, even though they were fake.

"Okay, that's enough hugging," Samantha said, who wasn't a slouch in the breast department; holding down some authentic 44 DD's.

She looked at Samantha and rolled her eyes.

"I promised my baby that I would behave if you brought this (she pointed to Samantha) with you. So

I'll ignore her ignorance today. It's a special day today."

"What makes today so special?"

"I can't ruin the surprise, Leonard."

"Looney or Looney Redz," he corrected Brandi. She grabbed his hand. "Come on hun."

Samantha followed them to the kitchen where it was a lot of food.

"Damn, who cooked all this food?"

"The best cook in our family cooked it," his father popped up and said.

Brandi ran to her man and kissed his lips, then squeezed his butt. Samantha made the throw-up face, and pointed to her mouth. Looney Redz smiled.

"It can't be Brandi. You told me she don't cook. It's not you, 'cause you don't cook. Lawrence is out in the streets somewhere. And Lisa is in Iraq. So who cooked the meal?"

"I was in Iraq."

Looney Redz froze at the sound of his sister's voice. "Turn around boy. It's me," Lisa said.

He turned around and looked into the green eyes of his sister, who he hadn't seen in three years.

Samantha looked at the drop dead gorgeous sister of her boyfriend, already having a vision of leaving Looney Redz for her.

Lisa Weathers looked just like her brothers. She was tall; 6'0", pretty emerald green eyes, small waist, thick hips, plumped 42" derriere, and set of 38 DD's you could get lost in.

Looney Redz hugged his big sister real tight.

"I know you missed me. I missed you too," she said. "Look at you. So handsome."

19

"Sis', this is—"

"I know who she is. I still got pictures of her and Lawrence," she scowled at her.

"Hoe!" Brandi coughed in her hand.

"Be nice," Loon whispered in her ear. She flashed him a toothy smile.

"She's my girl now, Lisa. Can you let it go?"

"Anything for my little brother," she said. "Hello Samantha. Nice to meet you."

"The pleasure is mine," she said, smiling. "He's told me so much about you."

She looked over at her brother and said, "Oh really. You telling stories again, baby brother?"

"Can we eat? The food looks like it's getting cold," he said.

"Wait. We can't eat without my baby," Lisa said, and went to the basement steps. "Come on baby! Time to eat."

"You brung ah nigga home, Lisa?" Looney Redz questioned.

"No, but if I did, I'm grown."

The kitchen was awkwardly quiet after Traum emerged from the basement.

"Everyone don't speak at one time," Brandi said, smiling.

"Fuck is he doing here?" Looney Redz jumped up from his chair.

"Now wait ah minute Leonard."

"Naw Pop, fuck that! I'm out. Lets go Sam."

"Don't do this Looney," Lisa said. "I let it go for you. Now put your differences aside for me. Please."

"Lisa, brother or no brother, I'm not sitting at no table with a rat."

"I keep telling you, I'm no rat."

"Nigga fuck you! Lisa, I'm sorry, I'm out. Lets go Sam."

"Sit down! Leonard Weathers, sit! Lawrence Weathers, sit down, now. Lisa Weathers, sit."

"I didn't do anything daddy," she said, and sat down. Both of her brothers did the same.

Samantha sat next to Looney Redz and assured him that she was with whatever he decided, by squeezing his hand.

"You two need to cut it out," Lisa said.

"Let it go baby-girl," her father said. "They'll work it out. Let's eat."

Forty-five minutes had past, everyone was full and warmed up. Everyone was talking, but not one word passed between the brothers. Looney Redz wasn't comfortable, at all, at the dinner table with his brother.

Tired of the absurdity amongst the two brothers, Loon decided to intervene.

"Ladies, can you excuse us for a while?"

"Sure daddy."

"Brandi, grab that 1949 bottle Richebourg Grand Cru Leroy," Loon said.

"The good stuff, huh? Lets go get drunk girls."

"What the fuck is wrong with you two?"

Neither one of them spoke up.

"So now y'all don't have shit to say?"

"I already said what the problem is. Ya oldest boy ah rat."

Traum sighed.

"You got proof of your accusations, son?"

"Yeah, the word on the streets," Looney Redz said.

"That's what's wrong with you young, stupid ma'fuckas now. Quick to slander someone's name because you don't understand or know a situation. See, back in my day, you called someone a snitch, you better have the proof on hand or it'd be you pushing up daisies from six feet under. You can't call someone a snitch and not know for certain. I wish you young mu'fuckas stop doing that. Paperwork isn't hard to obtain. Fuck what the next man or woman say. You never really know the motive of the gossiper. Bitch-ass niggas do bitch-ass shit for a lot of reasons. I once knew a bitch-ass nigga name Batman, who slandered a good man's name to anyone who'll listen. He didn't have no proof, no facts, no concrete evidence; just some fabricated stories. And the niggas that he's tellin' may have not believed him, but they carried the lie; so they're just as guilty. My point is, you have no proof that your brother is a rat. You running off of the words of the streets. Fuck the streets."

"Pops, he got locked up for two murders in—"

"Did you see him do it? Was you there?"

"No."

"Did you see it on the news?"

"No."

"Did you see any paperwork?"

"No."

"How do you know then Looney?"

"The streets," he whispered.

"I can't hear you," Loon said.

"The streets."

"I thought so," he said, and turned to his oldest child. "And you just as wrong for not telling him what really happened."

"I told you why I didn't tell him."

"Well, you need to tell him now. This bullshit has to stop," Loon said. "I'm going to get some of this three thousand-dollar bottle of wine before the girls drink it all. Y'all work it out."

They just stared at one another. Looney Redz was having conflicting feelings, now that his father dropped that jewel on him.

"You of all people lil' bro. I thought you'd take my word for it."

"Cut the shit Traum. If the shoe was on the other foot, I'd be dead right now."

"Bullshit! I wouldn't have done shit unless I was one hunnid times sure you was a rat. I'm incapable of telling."

"Everybody say that same shit, until they sitting on the other side of the table across from the FEDS, DEA, or some Homicide Detective, so miss me with that gangsta shit."

"That night, not day, that you think I got locked up for those two murders... I didn't. I never even got locked up period. I did have a gun on me, and two people did get murdered, but it wasn't me who did it."

Looney Redz looked at his brother not believing a word he said.

"Come on Looney. You know about every murder I did. Think about how do you know. How do you know?"

"Because you told me," he said. "A couple I seen myself."

"Exactly! So why wouldn't I tell you about two punk ass junkies that got killed? I didn't do it. I stumbled up on the shit," he said. "The police and Toe Taggin' was involved in the murders." The look of shock on his face told Traum that his brother really didn't know how deep this was. "Toe Taggin' Posse Music Group got the police on their side," Traum told his little brother. Then he gave him the whole story of what he saw and went through on the night of the murders.

"This shit crazy. So you thinkin' that the last recruit to Toe Taggin' Posse is fuckin' police?"

"I'm not thinkin' shit! I'm tellin' you that's what it is."

"We gotta tell'em."

"Fuck them niggas! Fuck'em all. We ain't tellin' them shit," Traum said. "I need a favor from you."

"What's up?"

"Remember that play I was telling you about that would affect everyone on the label?"

"Yeah, I remember."

"Well, I did it… but the shit went all wrong."

"What'chu mean, Traum?"

"The kidnapping. It went wrong."

"What does that have to do with Slaughtermore?" Looney Redz asked.

(Sighing) "I kidnapped 4Hunnid."

Looney Redz's eyes got big. "4Hunnid Ru?"

"Yeah."

"That's why he been MIA? Oh shit, Toe Taggin' don't want the public to know, so they been feedin' them with some bullshit about 4Hunnid being out of town. Where is he now?"

"I don't know," he said, shaking his head. "I asked for three Hunnid thousand. I had the shit in my hands!

I just had two idiots helping me. I had Dun Deal watching 4Hunnid, and a white boy name Meff with the money. They paid that money quick for 4Hunnid. I went to check on Dun Deal and 4Hunnid, and found the police all over the spot. Dun Deal was dead and 4Hunnid was carted off to the hospital. Then I go back to the house where the white boy and the money was at and find the bitch shot up. No sign of the money or white boy. Three hunnid thousand gone, just like that. I had it in my hands!"

"What do you need from me?"

"I need your help getting out of here. I need some money to get to Mexico."

"Huh?"

"4Hunnid know it was me. The rest of them probably know right now. I can't get caught slippin'."

"Give me a few weeks. Just stay low here with Pops and Lisa," Looney Redz said. "My bad about not believing you."

"It's aiight. This is some deep shit. I ain't ever been in no shit like this before."

"I got'chu bro."

CHAPTER 20
Accomplice

The few weeks had flown past quickly. It was the end of March and Looney Redz wasn't anywhere near getting the money up for his brother. It took him a week to find a block and another week to find a good, solid, reliable, good product carrying plug. Once those two feats were accomplished, he started from the bottom, but the block was beginning to turn a profit.

4Hunnid was rolling around the city in a black, tinted up Acura TL that his aunt got him. He rolled through all of Traum's old hang out spots, to no avail. He wasn't necessarily looking for Traum, knowing he wasn't stupid enough to be out and about, but was looking for a clue as to where he was hiding.

Azarah had packed up a few suitcases and moved in temporarily, while she nursed her man back to 400%. She learned quickly that 4Hunnid hated doing anything repetitiously, that wasn't mandatory, like showering, brushing his teeth, eating, and working out. She had to remind him constantly to take his medication. He hated the cream his dermatologist prescribed for him so he purposely forgot to put it, so she made sure she rubbed him down with it every night. She wanted him to get back out to the world as much as everybody else. She was tired of being questioned and blamed for his disappearance.

The media and radio stations played on the rumor that there was a riff amongst the members and executives of Toe Taggin' Posse Music Group. The whole Toe Taggin' Camp stuck to the lie they were telling, but the media, fans, and radio stations wasn't buying it. They handled the pressure by working harder. They were focused on their upcoming show at Pier 6, that was happening on May 10th, a day before mother's day.

Nyse, Madd Lou, Wild Bill, Dummy Yummy, L Trigga, and Magik was making money hand over hand with the new dope they were selling. There was a drought over the rest of the city. Magik still made sure 4Hunnid got his cut. His money was dropped off to Connie Y every Monday.

***

4Hunnid was driving down Edmondson Avenue when he spotted the familiar female. He sat at the red light on Edmondson and Braddish Avenue bouncing around what he was thinking in his head. The way he was going about tracking down Traum wasn't working at all. He knew he would have to incorporate someone else in his plans, but someone other than his friends, girlfriend, or anyone at Toe Taggin' Posse Music Group. He needed someone who wouldn't ask any questions.

He smiled as the girl walked across the front of his car. The hoodie she had on made up his mind. On the front of the hoodie was a photo of him and her. The back read: 4Hunnid is Toe Taggin' Posse 4 Eva.

It made him proud to see that some people still believed in his loyalty. He listened to the radio every night and got online everyday, so he was well aware of what was being said.

Beeeep! A car behind him blew the horn interrupting his thoughts. He made a right on Braddish and slowed down along side of the girl. She looked at the car, trying to peer inside, but couldn't because of the 5% tints that covered the windows.

He saw the nervous look on her face, so he let the passenger side window down a little bit.

"Come ride with me."

She looked again. "Nigga please. I don't get into strange cars, with strange men. I don't even talk to strangers," she said, and stepped off.

He pulled up some more. "Kim, stop playing and get in the car girl."

She looked again. "Who you?" she asked.

4Hunnid forgot all about the 887 hoodie and Medium Aviator Gucci shades that he had on.

"It's 4Hunnid."

She ran to the car to get a closer look. "OH MY GAWD! OH SHIT! 4Hunnid!"

"Kim! Shut up and get in the car!"

She put her hands over her mouth, looked around, and got in the car. He rolled the window up and pulled off.

"Oh my gawd 4Hunnid. Where you been nigga?"

"Laid back, getting my voice back together."

"I knew they wasn't lying," she said, excitedly.

"I heard when you called up to the radio station and blasted everyone for poppin' shit," he said.

"4Hunnid, you know how I do. I don't play when it comes to you or my niggas from Toe Taggin' Posse."

"I appreciate that," 4Hunnid said. "Where was you going?"

"To the store to get my grandmother some cigarettes."

"Can you hang out with me? I need a big favor from you."

"Hell yeah I can hang. Anything, name it," Kim said.

"First, lets get ya grandmother those cigarettes. Matter fact, get her a carton," he said, pulling out a fifty-dollar bill.

Once he pulled off from in front of her grandmother's house, he got down to business.

"First thing first, you cannot tell anyone, not a soul, that you seen me, talked to me, or know where I'm at. Understand that?"

"Yup," she said, and motioned like she was zipping her lips.

"I'm dead serious Kim, Nobody."

"Okay," she said. "Tell me what'chu need me to do."

"Before I tell you, I need you to know, understand, comprehend, and agree to something."

"Anything," she said, confidently.

"What I need you to do, will ultimately lead to someone or someones losing lives," he said, and she didn't even blink. "I need to know if you are willing to get involved still, and if so, can you take what you know to your grave?"

She looked him in his eyes and said, "I was raised with six brothers. Two of them doing life plus twenty; Out Back. Two more doing ninety years and seventy years. I got on the stand for all four of their trials, as ah alibi witness, even though they weren't with me. I have one brother in the army, and my other brother was killed last year by a rat nigga. I know the rules of the streets. My brothers taught me well."

"So you in?"

"I'm in… 400%."

He sighed. "You've been known to be at all the industry parties."

"Yup, yup."

"So, what I'm asking of you won't be out of the ordinary. I need some information on Slaughtermore. I'm looking for Looney Redz. I need to know where he rests his head at."

"That shouldn't be hard at all. My homegirl Cashmere be fuckin' him."

"It may be harder than you think. I think him and his girl live together, so he might take her to a hotel. Then again, Samantha goes both ways, so he might take her home. Check it out for me."

"How will I get in touch with you?"

"You don't. I'll stop pass your grandmother's house everyday. I don't know what time though. Who else stay with ya grandmother?"

"My junkie uncle."

"Put'em up in a motel with his drug of choice. I need that house empty. Grandma can stay. I'll get her to call you if you're not there," he said, handing her a stack of money.

"Okay."

"I'll make sure you straight."

"Thanks, 4Hunnid."

"No, thank you."

***

4Hunnid's House...

He walked in his house to the smell of breakfast food. Two T's met him at the door. She had on a burgundy bandanna and a burgundy Polo shirt.

"What the fuck," he said, looking at his dog. "You let her put this shit on you?"

"Roof!"

"The bandanna can stay, but the shirt gotta go."

He walked in the kitchen where he found Azarah butt naked in a pair of Christian Louboutin seven inch, high heel Red Bottoms. He totally forgot about the Polo shirt and Two T's as his insides swirled and all the blood rushed to his manhood. It was a war going on inside of his Seven jeans.

"You like?" she asked, and twirled around smiling. The cat definitely had his tongue.

"Why did you take Two T's shirt off?"

That snapped him back. He took a swallow and said, "Why do she got it on in the first place?"

"She's a lady. She needs to look like one."

"And ah Polo shirt and ah bandanna would—" He stopped when Azarah pointed to Two T's feet. "You painted her nails?

"You mad?" she asked, making this cute affectionate face.

"Kinda hard to be mad at you, Sexy, when you in my kitchen naked, cooking in a pair of Red Bottoms." She smiled. She sashayed over to him and kissed his lips.

"Baby, I wrote two songs I need you to get on."

"Oh really."

31

"Really."

"What's the name of them?"

"Balenciaga Panties and Red Bottom Bandit." He smiled.

"Aiight, I got'chu. Answer this though. Why are you cooking breakfast at seven thirty at night?"

"I told you breakfast is my favorite to cook. I was cooking for me and Two T's. Do you want something else?"

"Naw, I'll have what y'all havin'," he said, and sat down in the chair. "Go to your room Two T's."

Two T's flew out of the kitchen. 4Hunnid watched his girl's every move and she moved around the kitchen like he wasn't even there.

He grabbed his crotch repeatedly trying to undo the awkwardness of his raging erection inside his Seven jeans. She caught him a few times and laughed. She began switching harder and harder until her walk became 'stank'.

Azarah bent over in front of the sink to grab the dish detergent, exposing a moist box to the penetrating eyes of her man. That was all he could take. Before she could stand erect, she had his erection inside of her.

"Agghhh!" she cried out, as he slammed himself inside of her.

Two T's ran in the kitchen and then right back out once she seen them.

4Hunnid put his hands on her shoulders and pulled on them forcefully with every stroke. It hurt his pelvis, but he didn't care. Her box was so wet it made farting noises with each thrust.

"Oh gawd... 4... Hun... nn... nnid! Shit!"

"Take it," he shot back.

"Sto...op. Le... lem... me dry... my... puss... pussy... up... some," she said, embarrassed by the noise her box was making.

"Let it fart," he said, and kept on thrusting, but harder.

"Ahh! Umm! Mmmm! Oouuu... It... hu... hurts... soo... ooo... go... good... ba... by! Umph! I'm... ahhhhh... shit! I'm... ahhh! Oh—"

She came so hard and so much 4Hunnid thought she peed on him. It poured down both of their legs. 4Hunnid
kept on thrusting.

After her orgasm subsided, she assisted by throwing it back on him. She lost the feeling in her legs afterwhile, so she pushed him in one of the kitchen chairs and rode him like that. In that position he had the opportunity to attack her succulent breast. He handled each breast with precision.

Moans of pleasure escaped her full lips as another orgasm rocked her body. Once she came down from her orgasm, 4Hunnid stood her up and bent her over the kitchen chair and finished her off, ending in both of them exploding in euphoria.

1 Hour Later...

They both were laid up in the bed, after another session of love making, watching BET JAMS. The animated, popular rapper Bobby Shmurda's video was playing.

4Hunnid was smiling throughout the entire video. "You miss it, don't you?" she asked, when the video went off.

"I do," he said, and he did. He missed performing more than he did selling dope. He felt much better in front of an audience, cameras, and on a stage.

"What are you waiting for then? Your boys are tough as nine inch nails, but a blind man can see that they miss you. Especially Lou and Magik. You gotta get back in the booth and on the stage with your boys."

"In a second."

"A second? Next week we sign our contracts for our show at the Pier Six Concert Pavilion. You need to be on the stage with us. It won't mean as much without you."

"Y'all will be just fine without me."

(Sighs) "You are so stubborn, you know that?" she said, in frustration.

"I'll hit the booth tomorrow and lay them verses down for your songs. They for your album or mixtape?"

"Gunz wants to do a mixtape, but Jerrod wants an album. He said there's no need for a mixtape, because everyone already know what I have. He believes the time is now."

"And what do you believe?"

"I feel the same way. Shaky Love has already sold seventy thousand copies on iTunes."

"The original or the remix?" he asked.

"The remix," she smiled. "The original song sold fifty thousand. It's no secret that you are the man, bae," she said, running her hands through his hair.

CHAPTER 21
Time 2 Pay Up

Pier 6 Concert Pavilion Office...

"Good afternoon," Tammy Gruden came out and spoke to her guest.

They could tell she was from money. It wasn't the diamonds she wore, the Vera Wang form fitting dress she had on, nor was it the Guiseppe Zanotti heels she wore. It was her aura, her demeanor, and her confidence.

"Can I get you guys something; a snack, something to drink—"

"No thank you, Mrs. Gruden," Jerrod said.

"You must be Jerrod," she asked, extending her hand.

"I am," he said, taking her hand and shaking it gently, but firmly to let her know he wasn't soft. A trick he learned in business 101. "And this is the CFO of my label; Amil DeCario, and the A&R Thomas Gunthry."

"Please to meet you all. I just love your hair Ms. DeCario."

"Thank you. Amil is just fine."

"My husband should be out shortly. He's on the phone with a few concert promoters."

"Concert promoters?" Jerrod questioned, and was mad at himself the moment the words left his lips.

"Yes, we have a lot of events planned for the summer. I just love the summer."

"Heyyy! Jerrod my man!" Thomas Gruden yelled, coming out of his office.

Jerrod stood up and shook his hand. "Tom. This is my CFO, Amil DeCario and my A&R; Thomas Gunthry." "Greetings to you both," he said, taken aback by Amil's beauty. "Step in to my office. I am, grab us something to drink."

"Yes dear."

"No need. We're okay Tom."

"Strictly business, huh. Still the same ole Jerrod."

They all sat down in his office. Tom pulled out some papers and sat them on the table.

"So what's the game plan, Jerrod?

"Me and my team has been throwing around some ideas, but right now my artists has been working on new material."

"Yeah. I know. One thing I admire about your crew is, their work ethics. No one works as hard as you guys."

"Thank you."

"As you already know, I like rap music. My wife hates it. I believe in expressing yourself in how you see fit. If that way so happens to entertain others, then so-be-it."

"I agree," Jerrod said.

"Back to me being a fan of rap. I follow it. I even got a Facebook, Twitter, and IG page under Swaggy T Ent."

"You're crazy Tom."

"I just love rap, Jerrod. You think I'd be accepted in the rap realm? A middle age white guy? Well anyway, being as though I follow rap, especially the city's talent, I have some concerns."

"What? Come on Tom. What concerns?"

"Concerns about your number one man not being able to perform."

"We don't, and never, had a number one man. We are a unit, with each member being equal. My artists will tell you that. Now which one are you referring to?"

"The crazy one. 4 Hundred?"

"Hunnid," all of them corrected him.

"What are your concerns, Tom?"

"I'm hearing that he's not apart of Toe Taggin' Posse Music Group. When me and my partners decided to get TTPMG, we were under the impression that we'd sell out tickets, and out of our lawn seats."

"And?"

"If all the members aren't there, we fear we won't sell out."

"You let us worry about that. We are more than capable of selling out Pier 6."

"Are you willing to put your money where your mouth is?" Tom asked.

"I am."

"Then you shouldn't have a problem with signing the revamped contracts. Here's a copy of it with the new entries highlighted."

Amil grabbed the contract and read it silently. She read over it twice more and then turned to Jerrod. "It reads, that if they don't sell out, then Toe Taggin' forfeits the agreed upon one hundred and thirty thousand dollars per member. If the show isn't sold out, each member will receive thirty thousand dollars."

"What makes you think we're gonna sign some bullshit contract like that? We get forty thousand each for doing small venues like The Hott Spot and Bamboo. You playing a vicious game... with vicious people."

"Hey, hey, hey," Tom said, holding his hands up in surrender. "What happened to you putting your money where your mouth is?" he asked, but Jerrod was too angry to respond. "The only thing the revamped contract insures is a great show. I'm positive that you will sell out every seat in the house. Shit, you guys sold out the Baltimore Arena. These contracts are to please my investors; not me, I can assure you."

Everyone was quiet for a few minutes. Jerrod was still fuming and wanted badly to reach over the desk and snap Tom's neck. He hated this part of being a legit CEO. He wasn't use to this type of fuckery.

"You said you're positive that we'll sell out Pier 6 and that these contracts are solely for the comfort of your investors?" Amil asked.

"That's correct."

"Sure?"

"I assure you it is," Tom said.

"Good, then it's settled. Time to insure us."

"What do you mean," he asked.

"You're positive we'll sell out; so are we. You put in these contracts, that if Toe Taggin' Posse Music Group doesn't sell out Pier 6, you'll add the one hundred thousand dollars in addition to the guaranteed thirty thousand dollars. Now put your money where your mouth is. Trust me, you won't be disappointed. We have the hottest rappers in the city right now and our affiliates are hot, so our show will be worth every penny."

"On top of all that," Tommy Gunz spoke up for the first time, "if you've been following the Baltimore rap scene and have seen our shows in person or even on Youtube, then you know Toe Taggin' Posse prides itself on outdoing our last. Magik always says we're like fine wine, we just get better with time. We will surpass our Area show and for that fact alone our show will sell out. The city of Baltimore loves us."

"I believe you. I will get my lawyer to draft up the new contracts and have them brought to the clothing store," he said, standing up. They stood up too. "Nice doing business with you," he said, extending his hand.

Jerrod was still fuming, but he still shook his hand.

Jerrod hit the steering wheel as hard as he could out of frustration, when they got inside of his Mercedes G-Wagon truck.

Amil massaged his shoulders from the back seat. "It's gonna be okay. The guys and Azarah are straight. We got our guaranteed money."

"Fuck that money! I would've gave them two hundred thousand ah piece to do the show. I just hate it when these motherfuckin', cock-suckin'-ass business men try to play me."

"Calm down, Jerrod. It's nothing. We got it straight. Forget him."

"She's right, Jerrod. Fuck'em. Lets see what the contracts looking like. We're still in control here," Tommy Gunz said.

"Are we?" Jerrod asked, and pulled off.

***

Kim's Grandmother's House…

Kim's grandmother, Mrs. Marie, let him in after he explained his friendship to her granddaughter. "She told me you'd be coming, baby," she said, and made her way back to her favorite chair.

The whole house smelled like stale foot and cigarettes. He recognized the smell because Kim, sometimes, smelled the same way. It was one of those smells that stayed in the pores of your clothes.

"You know what time Kim suppose to be here?"

"Shortly," she said, looking at him. "Take those sunglasses and hood off in my house young man."

"Yes ma'am," he said, and removed them.

"Oh Lord. Sweet Jesus. Look at all that long pretty hair," she sung. "Such a handsome boy," she said. The TV was on the stories, so he knew she wasn't getting up for a while.

"What's your name, sweetheart?"

"Fortune, and yours?"

"Mrs. Marie. You and my granddaughter mess around?"

"No ma'am. We're just friends."

"You said that awful quick. What, she's not good enough for you or something?"

(Laughs) "It ain't that Mrs. Marie. She cool—"

"Stay out here. My grandmother don't like me bringing company in her house. I'll be right back," they heard Kim say, from the hallway.

4Hunnid put his hood and shades back on. Mrs. Marie looked at him through squinted eyes.

Kim walked in and was shocked to see 4Hunnid sitting on her grandmother's couch.

"Who out there?" he asked.

"My boyfriend. You good."

"We need to talk," he told her.

"Hey Gammy."

"Chile please."

She rolled her eyes and turned to 4Hunnid. "Come on. We can go up to my room?"

Her room was even worse. It smelled so bad, he had to open the window.

"What the fuck is that smell?"

"I don't know. I don't live here, shit."

"What'chu got for me, Kim?"

"Damn, no hug, no hi, no nothing?"

"I don't have time for all of that shit. What'chu got?"

"Cashmere wouldn't tell me where he live. She thinks I want to fuck him."

"So she know?" he asked.

"I guess she do. She was bragging about him being a dope boy now."

4Hunnid laughed.

"I'm serious 4Hunnid, she ain't lying. I been knowing her since elementary school. She ain't never had no style or ever been with a street nigga. This bitch was braggin', rockin' a Gucci dress and Gucci heels."

"What that mean?"

"She's ah Converse wearing bitch. Target shopper. Flea market creeper."

"What else she say?"

"She was just boasting about Looney selling all this dope out Dutch Village."

"Did she say anything about meeting his family?"

"She said she met his big brother—"

"Where?" he said, a little too quickly and excitedly, causing her to look at him with a raised eyebrow.

"Calm down cowboy," she said.

"Fuck all that. I need you to get Cashmere to tell you where that house at. That's what's gonna get me back on the music scene."

"Okay, okay. I'll try again."

"Do that," he said, tucking his dreads behind his hoodie. He put his shades on, left out her room, and went out the back door.

***

Dutch Village…

Dutch Village was a small community of apartment complexes located on the Northeast side of Baltimore. It wasn't considered a bad area, but, a lot of section 8 recipients had apartments in the community.

4Hunnid was familiar with the area, because he knew two females that lived inside the complex.

He rolled through the complex looking for any activity. He figured, if Looney Redz was smart, he'd have a few apartments in the complex to run his dope business. But he didn't see Looney Redz as a smart person.

4Hunnid didn't see one person in none of the apartment courts, so he drove across the street to the shopping center. He saw a man panhandling in front of one of the stores. He parked the car all the way at the other end of the shopping center and walked back up to the panhandler.

"You got some change sir?"

"Yeah, but you gotta do something for me."

"Anything nephew."

"I need you to go cop me ah bag of smack."

The man looked at 4Hunnid, trying to see beyond the Marc Jacob shades.

"You get high?"

4Hunnid lifted the sleeve of his hoodie to show him the needles marks from his stay at Prince George's Hospital.

"Damn nephew, you spiking? I don't spike, but I sniff."

"Don't play me unc. I'm giving you enough to get both of us right, and I'll put two hunnid in ya pockets when you come back."

He looked at 4Hunnid again, trying to gauge his eyes. "Embarrassed huh? Don't want no one to know you gettin' high?" 4Hunnid ignored him. "I was the same way when I was yo' age. I let ah funky-ass hoe turn me out. How you get hooked, nephew?"

"You wan' trade war stories or you wan' get high as the moon?"

Just the thought made his mouth water. "I'm going. Where's the bread?"

4Hunnid pulled out a knot of money, peeled off one hundred dollars and gave it to the panhandler. "As soon as you get it and bring it back, I'll give you the two hunnid dollars and you can do as you please. But hurry up. I'm tryna get high."

He grabbed the money and headed towards the apartments on a mission. He was so focused on the task at hand, he didn't even notice 4Hunnid following him.

He followed him to the last court in the complex. The house sat two doors from the corner. Ironically, it was two doors down from one of his lady friends. From his location, he had an unobstructed view of the front door and with his perfect vision, he recognized Speedy the second he opened the door for the man.

Speedy looked around the court for anything out of place. He didn't see anything out of place, so he served the man and closed the door. 4Hunnid had saw enough. He jogged back to the shopping center and waited for the guy to come back.

"I got us ten nice bags nephew," the man said, excitedly when he walked up on 4Hunnid in the parking lot. "He wouldn't let me get eleven for a hundred."

"Keep'em unc. They yours," he said, handing him two hundred dollars. He looked up from the money and drugs to 4Hunnid.

"I'm going to jail, ain't I?"

"Unc, I ain't no cop. It's your lucky day. Now get lost and enjoy ya self."

He didn't have to tell him twice. "Thanks nephew."

4Hunnid sat in the Acura gathering his thoughts. Time was of the essence he knew, so there wasn't but a few avenues to explore. He started the car and didn't turn it off until he was in the parking lot that was before the dope house's parking lot.

He put an all black bandanna across the bottom half of his face, put some Nike gloves on his hands, neatly tucked his dreads under a knitted hat, and then pulled his hoodie over his head. He grabbed the chrome .45, with his Nike gloved right hand, from under the driver's seat.

He waited until the sun went down before exiting the car. He made his way out of the court, and over to the last court. The lights were on in the house; upstairs and downstairs.

His adrenaline and heart was pumping hard, as it always did when he was about to put in some premeditated work. He took a deep breath and crept up to the house.

There was no peephole on the two-story row home, which faired good for 4Hunnid. He knocked on the door. "Who the fuck—" was all Speedy got to say before his neck was grabbed, and a gun was jammed into his mouth; breaking a lot of teeth along the way. The tears appeared in his eyes immediately.

"Who else in this ma'fucka, pussy?"

"Mgmm ugh ghhh uuggh."

"What, bitch?" he asked, removing the gun from his mouth and putting it on his forehead.

"Nobody but ah bitch."

"Where Looney Redz at?" he asked, pushing him inside the door.

"Home."

"Tell me where home is."

"My house?"

"No scared nigga. Looney Redz's."

"He lives out Windsor Mill on Northgreen Road. The fifty-five hundred block. I don't know the exact address. Please let me go, man."

4Hunnid pushed him on the floor.

"Where's the bitch?"

"She upstairs in the bed."

"Where's the dope and money?"

"The money in the freezer. The smack in the trash can in the kitchen, and the notebooks is under the couch."

They heard someone walking down the steps. 4Hunnid moved over and grabbed the girl by her hair the second she touched the last step. He threw her on the floor next to Speedy.

She screamed when she saw what 4Hunnid had on. He was shocked to see the girl he use to sleep with. He snapped out of it and held a gloved finger to his lips. She got quiet quickly.

4Hunnid held the gun on them as he reached in the kitchen to grab the trash can. He emptied the contents on the floor. He saw the bundles of dope in the trash. He kicked them free of trash and then looked down at the girl. He didn't want to risk Chelsee recognizing his voice, so he motioned her to stand up, with the gun.

She reluctantly stood-up, with tears in her eyes. She felt like death was there.

"Please, don't kill me."

He motioned for her to empty the freezer. She did as he instructed. Once she kicked everything out the kitchen to where they were, she came back and got back on the floor next to Speedy.

Boom! Boom! Boom! Boom!

He held his finger up to his mouth to keep her from screaming. He went to the couch and pulled out three kilos that resembled notebooks. He came back, emptied the dope over the dead body of Speedy, picked the money up and pointed the gun at the girl. She didn't scream out or blink. She was in shock. 4Hunnid took off outside at full speed.

***

**Brooklyn Holmes Projects…
(the next morning)**

Madd Lou was up, six am, smoking his first blunt of the day, while his female friend laid in the bed, sleeping off the pounding her body excitedly took on the night before.

He grabbed the remote and started flipping through the channels until he saw the weather. He got excited just looking at the seven-day forecast. Spring was here.

BREAKING NEWS popped up on the screen. He turned the volume up.

Police responded to shots fired in this small court of the Dutch Village community in East Baltimore at eight twenty-two last night. When police arrived on the scene they found the EMTs trying to revive an unresponsive black male that looked to be in his late twenties.

An ID near the body revealed the identity of one Cedric Cardwall. Police immediately ran the name through the system and learned that Cardwall also went by Speedy and was a member, rapper, and hype man for a local rap crew by the name of Slaughtermore Records. Police aren't saying whether they have any suspects or if this is related to the shooting death of Sherman Tate; another Slaughtermore affiliate…

"What are you laughing and clapping for Lou?" the girl asked. "You loud as shit."

"Shut the fuck up and go back to sleep," he barked, and smacked her naked butt.

"Ouch! You come put me to sleep, nigga."

***

Central Police Station…

Lieutenant Druce Buetelli was leaving a meeting with the police commissioner when he saw Coppola, Travoski, and Jarvos.

"LT, we need a word with you," Coppola said.

"Sure. Let's go to my office."

He flopped down in his chair and sighed. "What's the problem, kids?"

"A member of Slaughtermore Records was murdered last night."

"Yeah, and? Come on Coppola, spit it out."

"We want this investigation."

Lieutenant Buetelli raised his eyebrow at the trio of hip hop cops. "I thought you guys were dead set on going after Toe Taggin' Posse."

"We believe it's related to our case," Erk said. Coppola made a face.

Buetelli didn't put his favorite officer under the gun by pitting her against her partners. He used another tactic.

"How so, Jarvos?"

"Lieu', Slaughtermore and Toe Tagging has been at each other's neck since twenty-twelve. Davenport is the number one suspect in Slaughtermore's affiliate, Sherman Tate's murder. He gets kidnapped, and almost killed, and now Cardwall."

"All circumstantial, Jarvos. I don't want you screwing things up with this Toe Tagging case. Stay on the assignments I gave— Speaking of which, weren't you all watching Toe Tagging?"

"I have my eyes on my man," Coppola said.

"Was you watching Davenport, Travoski?"

"Yeah," he lied.

"And?"

"He's still in the hospital, to my knowledge."

"Well, your knowledge isn't jack-shit! Davenport been checked out of the hospital," he barked. "And you Jarvos? What about Louis and Damon?"

"Still in Brooklyn Holmes selling narcotics."

"I know you two fucks are lying to me. Coppola, please don't let the deceitfulness of these two idiots wear off on you."

"I won't."

"If you would've had your asses on your assignments, instead of dicking around, you would know for sure if Toe Taggin' was involved. Now get back—"

Ring. Ring. Ring. Ring.

"Excuse me," Buetelli said, picking up the phone.

"Yes… I'm listening… Oh really… So they want a few of my guys?... Sure. I'll send them down. Thank-you. I appreciate the opportunity. I owe you one Lidia," he said, and hung up. "Lucky bastards."

All three officers looked at the lieutenant, waiting for him to say something.

"They have an eye-witness to last night's murder downstairs on the seventh floor."

"What does that has to do with us?" Coppola asked. "Go to the seventh floor. Find Detective

Molino. If he allows you to question the suspect, I don't want you two talking to the witness. Coppola, you do the talking. Don't fuck this up. Now leave my office. Later Coppola."

"Later, Lieu'."

"I expect a full report when you're done."

"Yes, sir," she said, and left.

CHAPTER 22
Work Calls

"I'm warning you now, Jarvos, when we get in here you better not say shit. You better not even flex a vein."

"Or what? You're gonna tell Lieutenant Buetelli on me?" he smiled.

"I'm not playing, Ernie. I'm serious. I'm the lead on this."

He held up his hands in a mock-surrender. "Okay, okay. I won't say or flex anything."

"Let's go."

They walked around the corner where Travoski and Detective Molino was standing by an opened door. "You all ready?" Molino asked.

"Yes. Thank-you for calling us in."

"No problem. I'll be in this room here looking and listening from the one-way mirror."

"Okay."

"Go."

The eye witness head was down when they walked in. "Excuse me," Coppola said. "Hi, I'm Detective Talia Coppola and this is my partner, Ernie Jarvos. We're here bec—"

"Please, not again. I already told this story four times already. My story hasn't changed any. Can I go home now? I'm tired."

"I need you to tell it one more time; for me. What's your name?" Coppola asked.

"Chelsee McGriff."

"Ms. McGriff, tell me what happened."

She sighed. "I was upstairs in the bathroom. When I came out, I heard someone ask Speedy where the dope and money was. That's when I came downstairs."

"Why not stay hidden upstairs?"

"I thought I recognized the voice."

"Who did you think it was?"

"A guy I use to mess with."

"What's his name?" Coppola asked.

"His nickname 4Hunnid or Zero To 4Hunnid In 4 Second Flat. His real name is King Tremaine Davenport."

"Why did you say 'you thought' it was him?"

"Because I did. When I got downstairs, I had a different thought. He wasn't built like 4Hunnid. His eyes were gray. It didn't look like he had dreads neither."

"What did the suspect have on?"

"Small details like that has escaped me. I know he had on a black hoodie; no distinguished patterns or words. His eyes were gray. He had on a black hat. He had a black bandanna tied around the bottom half of his face."

"He didn't sound like Davenport when you got downstairs?"

"That's the thing. He didn't say one word when I got downstairs. Nothing. He gave orders with his gun."

"That didn't seem odd to you?"

"No, not at first. But once I thought about it, it did."

"So could it have been that he was being quiet, because he knew you?"

"Yup, it could've been," she said. "Or it could've been one of the guys around the neighborhood."

"Or Davenport."

"I don't believe it was him. Nothing fit for it to be him. Trust me, I've been all over that body."

"Did you notice anything about the suspect's movements? Like, was he limping, holding his side? Did he look hurt in any way? Think. This is very important."

She thought long and hard about it. She remembered watching him run out the door.

"He might've had a slight limp to his run. I couldn't swear on it, but I believe so."

Coppola thought long and hard about her next question. "What was your relationship to the deceased?"

"We were friends," she cried, remembering all four shots he took to his face.

"It's okay. We're gonna find whoever did this. We just need your help." She nodded her head. "Who else frequents that home?"

Chelsee knew the harder questions were coming, she just didn't know they were coming so soon. She wasn't trying to get none of her friends-with-benefits in trouble. "Don't think about your answer, Chelsee," Erk said. He just couldn't sit quiet any longer. "Answer the question with the truth. Lying will only get you in trouble Sit on that."

She looked at Erk through teary eyes.

"Who else be in the house, Chelsee?" Coppola asked.

Rick Flare and Looney Redz. I don't know their real names."

"Leonard Woathers and Gerald Evergreen are their names. The home isn't in any of their names, so they're just using the house to pump drugs out of?"

She shrugged her shoulders. "I don't know."

"I'll give you that, but I know you know. You're a bright girl."

Coppola questioned Chelsee for another hour, with Erk giving his two cents more often than not, and then left out with five pages of notes. Jerk was outside waiting on them. The look on his face told them something was up.

"What's up Travoski?" Erk asked. He pointed to the door him and Detective Molino walked out with a red faced Lieutenant Bruce Buetelli. Erk knew he was in trouble.

"In my office; all three of you in twenty minutes," he said, and stormed off.

"I told you not to say anything. Now you done fucked up," Coppola said. Erk walked off, ignoring her.

***

Toe Taggin' Attire…
Dee Dee was training the two new cashiers that she hired when the police and two detectives stormed

the store. She discreetly hit the store's panic button, to alert everyone in The Dungeon.

"We have a warrant to search the premises," Detective Lin said, holding up the piece of paper.

Dee Dee stepped from behind the counter to examine the warrant. "Excuse me, but I need to view that warrant before you start walking around **my** store."

He handed her the warrant and it didn't take long for her to find a problem.

"Y'all do not have a warrant to search **my** store. Y'all have a questioning warrant for a King Tremaine Davenport. He does not live in here. This is a place of business, so could you please leave?"

"Davenport frequents this establishment."

"So. He's not here."

Jerrod came from the back of the store. "Can I help you?"

"Not unless you know where King Tremaine Davenport is."

"I'm afraid I don't."

"What's your name?"

"Jerrod Frampton."

Lin went in his pocket and pulled out a piece of paper.

"You were next on my list of people to talk to. Where you wanna do this, here or downtown?"

"We can do it on the moon, as long as my lawyer is present."

"I'll give you a chance to call your lawyer before we leave," he told Jerrod. "He's going with us boys."

***

"Suspended without pay and I'm off the case! This is bullshit!" Erk yelled, when they got to the parking lot. He kicked over a nearby trash can.

"This is why. You can't control yourself. Those steroids are fucking your brain up, Jarvos. You need help."

"Fuck that, and fuck you too," he said, and stormed off.

"He's got some serious issues."

"Tell me about it, Travoski. Why don't you ever say anything to him?"

"The guy is fuckin' crazy Coppola. I don't want to have to shoot him."

"So what's our next move, Travoski?"

"We go find Weathers and Evergreen."

***

Windsor Mills, Maryland...

4Hunnid was sitting on the fifty-five hundred block of Northgreen Road in the Acura, with his eyes wide open, looking for any clue on where Looney Redz's house was. He wasn't four hundred percent sure that Speedy was telling the truth because the houses looked out of Looney Redz's price range, but it was the only thing he had to go off of.

Twenty minutes of sitting still, he saw a tall, big butt woman come out of 5503 Northgreen. 4Hunnid sat up in the car. He strained his eyes to get a good look and smiled.

He quickly wrote something on a piece of paper and hopped out of the car. He began looking around like he was lost. The woman took one look at him and knew he wasn't from the area.

"Excuse me, you lost?" she asked.

He smiled that sixty-thousand dollar smile and hooked her. "I am. I'm looking for this street here," he said, handing her the paper.

"Oh, Southgreen Road is four blocks over." She handed it back, but instead of just grabbing the paper, he grabbed her hand with it, causing her to blush.

"You got a pretty smile, you know that," he said.

"Is that all," she flirted.

"Yup, that's it."

She laughed out loud. "Well, I gotta go. See you around," he said, and walked away.

Her smile turned into a frown when he turned to walk away. She wasn't use to being turned down; especially when she initiated the flirting. She was upset, but it also turned her on, and being in Iraq for three years, with only her toys and memories, his actions had her box on fire.

So she did something she hadn't done in her entire thirty-four years of living; chase.

"Excuse me," she said, stopping him from closing his door. "What's your name?"

"KT and yours?" he asked, from the driver's seat.

"Lisa."

He extended his hand. "Nice to meet you Lisa."

"You in a hurry?"

"Kinda. You wanna go out to dinner tonight?"

"Where?" she asked.

He thought about it. "Kobe's Japanese Steakhouse."

"The one out Largo, Maryland?"

"Ugh un. The one out in White Marsh," he said, smiling

"Okay."

"Can you meet me there at nine tonight, Lisa?"

"Sure. I'll see you then," she said, and walked off, making sure he got a glimpse of her phat backside. She looked back and saw him shaking his head.

"This shit don't make no sense how much these motherfuckers look alike." 4Hunnid drove off laughing to himself.

***

4Hunnid's home…

Azarah was in the bed when he walked in the room. He started taking off his clothes.

"The police ran up in Toe Taggin' Attire today and grabbed Jerrod."

"You know why?"

"They had a questioning warrant for you."

"What?"

"You gotta call Connie Y for all the details, because that's all I know. You know how secretive y'all is." He walked to his house phone and called his aunt

"Yarborough and Associates, can I help you?"

"Can I speak to Connie Y? This 4Hunnid."

"Hold on."

"Hello, nephew?" she said, when she came to the phone.

"Yeah, this me. What's up?"

"They questioned Jerrod about your kidnapping. They talked to Magik too. We mostly listened to them talk shit and make idle threats. They said they want to

58

question you about the murder of one of those Slaughtermore boys."

"Why me?"

"They have reason to believe it's connected to your kidnapping."

"Bullshit."

"I agree."

"What's your advice?"

"Get rid of the Acura and lie low."

"You know I can't do the second one," he said, looking at Azarah, who was staring him dead in his face.

"Well be careful, 4Hunnid. We are going to have to face Lin sooner or later."

"We will, but not now. I'm not tryna keep going to see them every time something happens."

"Just be careful. I love you."

"Love you too," he said, and hung up.

"Everything okay, bae?"

"Yeah," he said, and headed for the shower.

***

(8:50 p.m.) Kobe Japanese Steakhouse...

4Hunnid walked in the restaurant dressed in a white YSL sweater, YSL jeans, and a pair of YSL hightop sneakers. His dreads were tied in two neat ponytails.

He spotted Lisa immediately. She smiled when he walked up and stood to hug him.

"Looking good... and smelling even better. Ooo, what's that smell, KT?"

"It's Yves Saint Laurent La Nuit de L'Homme."

"And you speak French?"

"No I just know how to pronounce things," he laughed. "You looking good yourself," he said, eyeing her body in the form fitting backless dress she had on.

"Thank-you."

A waiter approached. "Are you all ready to order?"

"Yes," he said. "Ladies first."

"I'll have the Kobe fried rice, and the seafood combination."

"Give me the filet mignon, and lobster please."

"Sure. What would you like to drink?"

"The house wine is fine."

"Okay, sir."

The chef came over to their table and fried the rice on their tepanyaki table.

"Tell me about you."

"I guess I should now, because wine turns me into a totally different person," she giggled.

4Hunnid wanted to spit in her face.

"Let's see… I'm thirty-four, I love working out, I'm very outgoing, I love having fun, I'm in the army—"

"What made you go to the army?"

"Growing up with two knucklehead brothers would run any girl off."

"The army, though? Why not college on the west coast? Why not a beauty school far from here? Why not modeling in New York?"

She blushed. "I'm too much of a tomboy to be a model."

"Could've fooled me. I don't see a stitch of tomboy in you."

"You gotta see me on Sunday with my father around the house with my Big Ben jersey on."

He twisted his face up. "A Steelers fan? Come on Lisa."

"I guess you're a dirty bird fan?"

"All day and tomorrow."

"We're gonna have to make a bet the next time they play. You name it, any-thing you want," she flirted. 4Hunnid smiled. The chef sat two plates of steaming fried rice in front of them. At the same time, their entrees showed up with their wine.

Everything about Lisa was sexual. The way she ate her seafood. The way she used her tongue to eat the shrimp, to the way she down the three glasses of wine. She was tipsy and very talkative by the end of their meal and 4Hunnid was getting antsy. He had extracted all the information he needed out of her and was now trying to find a way to ditch her.

She sobered up some when the air hit her outside. "Can we sit in your car for a few, so I can sober up?"

He started to say no, but he didn't. "Come on."

When she got into his car, her dress mysteriously hiked more than half way up her thick thighs.

"You know about me KT, but I don't know anything about you. It's your turn."

"Just listen," he said, and pushed a button on the touchscreen system of his Jeep Cherokee.

Yeah, I pop a lot of shit, thinkin' of keepin' it moderate Me and mine been iced out, hoppin' out of shit Right now I'm praying for my nigga to get this scholarship
A nice university, one of those black colleges
Far as the hood go, I acknowledge it
But whoever ain't a snake usually a follower

Luckily, I can tell the difference
My big homie doing 38, my other homie gettin'
sentenced
Bitch niggas usually send the hate through the
bitches Jealous Instagram niggas hating on your
pictures Toe Taggin' paper chasin', y'all niggas
walking behind wishes
Without working for it, y'all niggas gon' remain
bitches Some niggas find coffins, others just find
ditches Just ask around about the Toe Taggin' militia,
they malicious
Sellin' dope, finish that and cop more dope
I'm four stroke, you'bout to stroke
If you got enough cigars we can all smoke
Ain't nothin' all good when you all broke
So we could never be equal
Never bite the hand that'll feed you
Never fear a man if he bleeds too
Some niggas need a head shot, some niggas need
two Play sweet in these streets and they'll leave you
You can't see the devil, he's see through
4Hunnid!

"Who was that?"
"Me."
"You lying."
"Dead ass," he said.

She leaned over and undid his pants. A few pulls on him and he was at full staff. She proceeded to suck him to the best of her ability. He reached over and pulled her dress all the way up over her butt and stuck two fingers into her wet folds. She screamed out on him as his fingers moved in and out of her.

He felt himself getting to the point of no return, so he removed his fingers and stuck them in her butt. That caused her to act-ah-fool on his tool. She moved up and down, faster, and faster, until he released his daycare in her mouth. She swallowed every drop he had to offer and didn't come up until she was sure he was clean.

4Hunnid wasn't done yet though. He removed his two fingers from her butt and placed them to her lips. She cleaned his fingers as well. He grabbed some baby wipes from the middle console and did the rest of the job on his hands and handed it to her when he was done.

"I'm never gonna see you again, am I?"

"Of course you are. That's my word you are." She had tears in her eyes. "What's wrong?" he asked.

"You must really be thinking I'm a freak, don't you?"

"Not at all," he smiled, calming her fears. "You saw something you wanted, and set out to get it. That's my type of woman. I'm the same way. I go after what I want."

"Thanks for dinner," she said.

"Write your number on this paper. I'll see you soon beautiful."

She wrote her number on the paper and got out of the car.

***

4Hunnid found Azarah laid across the bed, fully clothed when he walked into his room.

"What's up, Sexy?"

"Don't what's up me, nigga. Are you cheating on me?"

"Yeah. No. It's complicated."

She was up off the bed faster than either one of them expected. "What the fuck did I tell you nigga?!"

"I only got the head, but it was important to my mission to let it go down the way it did."

She looked at him like he had six heads on his shoulders.

"Are you fuckin' serious right now?"

He sighed. *I'm telling the truth*, he thought, *why doesn't she understand, this relationship shit is harder than I thought.* "I don't know what to tell you. I did what I did because I had to."

"Okay, cool. Let me go out and let some nigga suck my pussy, and then come home and tell you it was important to my mission to let him suck my pussy."

"That would be some other shit, because you not on no mission, Sexy."

"My motherfuckin' name is Azarah! Not Sexy! Call that bitch that sucked your dick, sexy!"

"Calm down, Azarah. It ain't like that, trust me."

"Then tell me what it's like. What's this mission?"

"I can't tell you right now, Azarah."

"Fuck you, 4Hunnid! I'm outta here!" she said, and started grabbing her things.

"You ain't going nowhere."

"Yousa lie! Fuck you!"

"Two T's!" he called out. Two T's showed up at the doorway of his bedroom immediately. "If she tries to leave, bite her ass."

She tried to leave out the door, but Two T's jumped up and snapped at her neck. She fell back, appalled.

"Yeah, straight for the jugular vein," he said.

"So you gonna keep me in here, King?" she cried. He took his clothes off and headed for the shower. Azarah looked at Two T's, who was staring her down. "Bitch," she said, getting up off the floor.

Two T's growled, showing her sharp canines.

PART 3

WHAT GOES UP

MUST COMES DOWN

CHAPTER 23
Slaughtered More

Two Days Later...

4Hunnid was on day two of watching Looney Redz's house. He knew from the drink, motor mouth, that all of her siblings were living under one roof. He was tempted to just rush the house, but he didn't want to kill anyone but Traum. He wanted his old life back bad and he knew that wasn't possible with Traum still breathing.

Just when he was about to let his thoughts turn to his woman, Loony Redz's front door opened. Looney Redz and Lisa came out the house. They walked to his Benz.

Traum came out of the house, at the same time, an unmarked police car turned down their block. 4Hunnid stood up with the SR9C .9mm Lugar Extendo, that held 33 and 1 in the head.

He took off full speed towards Traum. Traum felt the grim reaper near and snapped his head up. He couldn't tell who was coming, but it didn't matter, someone was on him.

Boom!

Lisa screamed. 4Hunnid ran pass the Benz in pursuit of Traum; who was hauling ass. The car that was coming down the street sped up in pursuit of them both.

Boom! Boom! Boom!

"Shit!" 4Hunnid yelled. The pillows and extra clothes he had on was slowing him down, but he was still running. He knew Traum would slow down some soon.

Boom! Boom! Boom! Boom!

The last shot hit Traum in the leg, sending him crashing to the ground face first.

4Hunnid ran over to him. "Bitch, you had to know I was coming. Pussy-ass Slaughtermore nigga."

Boom! Boom! Boom! Boom! Boom!

Scarrrrrrd!

"Freeze!"

4Hunnid turned around firing, sending the officer crashing to the ground for cover. He shot the cop's tires out, shot Trauma three more times, and made his escape.

***

Lisa and Looney Redz was in two different rooms at Central Police Station. Talia Coppola questioned Lisa and Looney Redz. They gave the description of who they saw, but wasn't much help in any other aspect of the investigation. Looney Redz refused to answer any questions about Slaughtermore and Toe Taggin' Posse's beef.

They were all in the lieutenant's office.

Lieutenant Buetelli looked at Detective Ernie Jarvos in a disgusting manner. Jarvos' badge and gun laid on the lieutenant's desk.

"Don't fire him LT."

"Give me one good reason, Coppola?"

"He's a big part of our team, LT. Look how many cases we've solved. No other team inside of IITS Unit solved more cases than us. Give him another chance, please."

"What do you think, Travoski?"

"Yeah Lieu', give him another shot. We need'em. Toe Taggin' is getting sloppy, and this case is almost over."

"Tell me, Jarvos, why were you at the Weathers residence? Even after I suspended you without pay."

"I'm sorry, Lieu', but I felt that something was gonna go down."

"You were right and almost got yourself killed," he said. "I gotta say, I love your dedication, but Jarvos, you can be down right stupid sometimes." The lieutenant sighed. "I'm gonna give you one last chance Jarvos, because you are a good cop. You're just stupid sometimes," he said. "So tell me, what's going on?"

"We have to find this shooter," Coppola said.

"And it's definitely not Davenport?"

"I'm positive, lieutenant. I got a good look at his body type. Unless our boy put on some weight, and cut his hair. It's the same guy that Ms. McGriff gave a description of."

"Then why are you so sure it's not Davenport? The way McGriff described the perp, was that he was clothed real good. The same way you're saying he was. All this is telling me, is that this perp went through extreme measures to not be seen or recognized and who would go through such measures?"

"Someone who everyone knows," Travoski said. "Bingo! Now go get Mr. Davenport, and deny him his lawyer for a few hours."

***

Brooklyn Holmes Projects...

Madd Lou, L-Trigga, Nyse, and Dummy Yummy was smoking themselves silly. The room was so cloudy, you could barely see.

"Where the fuck is this nigga, Lou?"

"Relax Nyse. Boy you don't have no patience. The nigga said he'll be through soon. It ain't like we got phones."

The door swung open and in walked the owner of the house.

"Yo, it's ah nigga and ah bitch outside looking for Madd Lou, with guns out! Look out the window!" They all ran to the window. Sure enough, there was a man and a woman outside, but guns wasn't what they had. Assault weapons was the proper term.

Madd Lou and L-Trigga smiled, and went to the door. The dread head, Mossberg 715P Semi-Auto toting man faced Madd Lou smiling.

"Fuck is up boy?"

"Man, put that shit up before somebody call the police. Who is she?"

"My ex-wife. Go get the stuff baby."

"Okay."

"Come on Lou. Where the fuck Trigg at?"

"I'm right here. Fuck is you doin' out here wavin' guns an'shit like you crazy?"

"Shit man, you young niggas nuts. I don't trust shit under thirty-three. I 'on't even trust my own kids and they only four and six. You should see me with the Mac II at breakfast making their sandwiches for school."

They all broke out laughing and embraced.

Ten minutes later they were all sitting around the kitchen table with a large suitcase on top.

"Before we get down to business, Boo-Boo, these are my homeboys Nyse and Dummy Yummy. Yo, this Boo Boo and his ex-wife."

Dummy Yummy spoke, Nyse didn't. Boo-Boo eyed Nyse suspiciously.

"I gotta watch this one," he said, pointing to Nyse. "Keep ya eye on the mohawk," he told his ex-wife.

"Let's get down to business, can we?" L-Trigga said, not really feeling comfortable with being in the projects conducting this type of business.

Boo-Boo stood up and opened the suitcase. The assortment of guns made them drool.

"Welcome to my shop motherfuckers!" Boo-Boo yelled. "Since I consider you two family, every one you get, I'll comp you a matching extendo."

They all started picking up guns, getting the feel for them. Nyse had forgot all about not liking Boo Boo once he started finger fucking all those beauties.

After an hour, Dummy Yummy had chose a Ruger LCR .357 Magnum Revolver, Madd Lou chose the CZ USA 75 Shadow 9 mm, Nyse grabbed two FN Herstels, and L-Trigga Picked the HK45 .45 ACP.

"I see you've made your choices," he said. His ex-wife closed the suitcase and left out.

"Yo, why do you travel with your ex-wife?" Dummy Yummy asked.

"She's the best shooter I know. She could shoot ah apple off ya head, in the rain, at night, no street lights, no glasses, standing still, with both eyes open—"

"We got it Boo-Boo. How much we owe you?" L Trigga asked.

He looked at the guns they were cradling and did the math mentally. "Give me thirty-five and they're yours." They paid him and he got up to leave.

"Wait," Nyse said. "Where is the clips and bullets?" (Laughs) "Come on young boy, I am a gun dealer, I'm not stupid."

"Man, where y'all find this weird-ass nigga?" Nyse asked.

"The correct question would be, where did y'all find this cautious-ass nigga. See y'all around and be safe. Remember, guns don't kill people, people kill people." Boo-Boo waved, pulled his assault weapon out and left out.

"Where y'all know that nigga from?"

"That's 4Hunnid'd man. We been buying guns from Boo-Boo for years and his way of doing business never changes."

"So where is the clips and bullets, Madd Lou?"

"He not gon' ever sell you bullets, Nyse, but the clips should be on the steps in a bag."

"Bullshit," Nyse said, and went to the door. He came back to the kitchen with a big brown paper bag. The clips that came out of the bag were all brand new, just like the guns.

"Oh yeah. Regulars and extendos," Nyse said, excitedly.

"It's on," DY said.

"Aiight, we ready for it. Now, how we gon' do it?"

"That's why we here, Trigga."

"I say we—"

Everyone held their hand up to stop Nyse from talking. "Sorry, baby boy," L-Trigga said, "not this time. We gotta get away scott-free with this one. No runnin', no shootin' at the police, no none of that."

"Come on yo, 4Hunnid havin' ah blast out there layin' them bitch-ass niggas down. Why don't we just choose ah nigga an' take'em out? That's all I was gon' say."

"That ain't ah bad idea, bruh," Madd Lou said.

Nyse could see everyone was thinking about his idea. He smiled, knowing his idea was more about him, than anything. He had two twin FN's and two extendos, he didn't want his homeboys over his shoulders telling him to calm down or chill. He wanted free reign to do whatever he wanted to do.

"I got Rick Flare. I owe that bitch," Nyse said. They all looked at him.

"Me and Bill will take BK," Madd Lou said.

"I'll get Polar Bear," L-Trigga said. "It's gon' take this HK to bring his big-ass down."

"I guess that leaves me with Fry," Dummy Yummy said. "Let's kill these niggas and get back to the money. I'm up to seventy ah day on Shirley Ave."

"Let's go. Fuck is we still talking for," Nyse said.

***

4Hunnid's House... (three days later)

It was five days later and Azarah was still in the house; stuck. She hadn't said two words to him since he gave Two T's the order to watch her. It didn't bother him at first, because he was focused, but now that all debts were settled, her silence was bothering him. She dressed in skimpy clothes and sexy under garments just to tease him. She satisfied herself to sleep by smiling at the front of his boxer briefs.

He walked upstairs, sat the bag he was carrying by the door and went in the room. Azarah was laying across the bed in a red La Perla panty set. The bottoms did a poor job of concealing her butt.

"What's up, Sexy?" he asked, but she ignored him. He got on the bed with her, leaned over, and tried to kiss her, but she turned her face.

"You still on that?" He sighed. "Come on yo. Stop being mad."

Two T's made a noise on the other side of the bed, on the floor.

"Two T's go."

"Roof!" she barked, and left the room.

He walked out the room, grabbed the bag, and came back in the room. Her eyes locked in on the big Herm̄s shopping bag.

"I got you some stuff. Here."

She didn't budge.

"Come on, Sexy. I got you a Hermēs bag, Versace earrings and a ring, some Bottega Veneta pumps and—"

"Can I leave?" she finally said.

"That's what the silence is about?"

"Can I leave?" she asked, more forceful.

"Yeah, my business is over with."

She hopped up quickly, threw on a pair of True Religion jeans, her Jordan 13's, and was gone in a flash.

"This is what a relationship is all about," he said, and laid back on the bed. "No wonder I stayed single."

***

Toe Taggin' Attire...

As soon as she walked through the door, Dee Dee's eyes dug into her.

"What?"

"Where have you been for the past week, girl?"

"I'm sorry Dee-Dee. This was out of my control," Azarah said.

"Girl, you can't be pulling disappearing acts around here, with all the shit that's going on out in the streets."

"Like what?"

"Guess you haven't seen the news either?"

She shook her head.

"Girl, them Slaughtermore niggas been droppin' like flies. First someone chased Traum down and shot him up; killed him. Then they found Polar Bear's body downtown with his head cracked open; dead. BK's body was found tortured and burned in front of his sister's house. It's just been a big-ass mess. Then we were trying to call you and your phone was going straight to voicemail."

"I'm sorry. I'm really sorry. It won't happen again. I need to get in the booth. Is anyone around?"

"Magik, Jerrod, Train, Madd Lou, Wild Bill, Tommy Gunz, Trina, and Amil is locked up."

"For what?!"

"Nothing. They're being held for questioning, Connie Y said. Since they all couldn't be represented by her office, she had to contact a friend of hers name Kia Perry."

"Kia Porry is the shit. She beat a lot of big cases."

"I know. So she got half of them and Connie Y's firm has the other half."

"What about me and 4Hunnid? They're not looking for us, are they?" Azarah asked, knowing they wasn't looking for her or she would've known.

"They didn't say anything about you. Probably because you're still new to the family, but Mr. Hunnid is their number one priority. They still got people—" Two plain clothes officers walked in the store. "… watching the store," Dee Dee finished.

"Good evening ladies. Ms. Brown, we were in the neighborhood and wanted to stop by to see if Mr. Davenport showed up."

"The answer is the same as the last fifteen times y'all were in the neighborhood; no."

"You look familiar miss. What's your name?"

"It's none of your business what my name is."

"You wanna go to jail with your smart mouth miss?"

"Just tell'em your name girl. I don't need everyone in jail," Dee Dee said.

"Let me see some identification," the officer said.

She removed her LV wallet from her MK bag and handed it to the officer.

"Queen Azarah Williams," the officer said, and grabbed his walkie talkie. "I need a warrant check on a Queen Azarah Williams. That's Queen, apple, zelda, adam, roy, alex, happy, Williams."

"*Stand by*," the officer on the other end said.

"We know who you are, Soulful. R&B queen of Toe Taggin' Posse Music Group. Alleged girlfriend of King Tremaine Davenport. Have you seen your boyfriend?"

"I don't have a boyfriend," she shot back.

"Well, have you seen your label mate?"

"No, I haven't. He's still out of town."

"Bullshit! You and everyone else in this building knows he's not out of town. I'm not a fan or a family member, as you all affectionately call them. We know 4Hunnid is on a revenge trip to kill everyone involved in his kidnapping. We need to find him before anyone else gets hurt."

The officer who called in her name stepped away from them to answer his cell phone.

"You don't have nothing to say?"

"I don't know what the fuck you talking about."

"You must want to join the rest of your label downtown. I'm pretty sure Amil and Trina could use some company."

"You ain't taking me no motherfuckin' place!"

The other officer rejoined them. "Come on, she's clean."

"Her mouth is dirty though. I'm about to arrest her on disorderly conduct."

"Let it go, Miles. We have somewhere else to be. Let's go."

"What?"

He handed Azarah back her belongings. "Let's go, Miles," he said through clenched teeth.

"Girl, you are crazy!" Dee Dee exclaimed. "You are just like my baby, 4Hunnid. He talks shit to the police just like you. Y'all are so much a like."

"They get on my nerves. Now I need a blunt. You got some weed?"

"Yeah. I still got that strong shit you gave me. That shit is too strong. You want it?"

"More so I need it," she said.

"I like the way you handled the cops," Dee Dee said, as she went to lock the door.

Twenty minutes later Azarah was in The Dungeon inside of the studio smoking a big blunt. She had the tracks from her album playing in the background.

Now that she knew the police was looking for 4Hunnid for all of those murders, she was no longer mad at him. Worry settled into her body for her man.

***

4Hunnid was surfing the 'net reading all of the articles on the recent string of murders of the Slaughtermore rap crew. He smiled as he read the articles, knowing his homeboys was responsible for the carnage.

In between reading the articles, he tried calling his aunt, but was unsuccessful. He figured with all the killings going on, now was the time to turn himself in for questioning. He knew they'd try to keep him for the full allotted twenty-four hours, so he wanted his lawyer/aunt on point.

After not being able to reach his aunt for an hour, he went to one of his favorite internet hip hop shows;

D. Rose Hip Hop Show. Ironically, she was playing one of their songs; *Family Over Everything.*

Come on 4Hunnid, where are you? Damari said, once the song went off. *We miss you, your energy, and your lyrics. Get at us.*

Speaking of 4Hunnid, I know y'all seen the news today. If you haven't let me be the first to bring you this Breaking News.

At ten a.m. this morning, authorities ran in ten residents looking for members of the Toe Taggin' Posse Music Group. They were able to apprehend the CEO; Jerrod, the CFO; Amil, both Trojan Boyz; Madd Lou and Wild Bill, Train, the A&R Tommy Gunz, one half of the Wild Hunnids; Magik aka 2 Hunnid and his wifey Trina.

I guess the good sign is none of them has been charged with anything. Let's say our prayers for them and the lives that were lost.

4Hunnid sat up in the bed and ran his hands through his hair. This was bad. With everyone locked up, he knew who they'd be looking for next, if they couldn't get him; his girl.

He was on the road in twenty minutes, driving a rented Chevy Tahoe XLT, listening to Madd Lou's mixtape; *Fuck Ya Life: Cherry Hill Edition.* He felt naked in the SUV without his gun, but he knew he couldn't ride dirty with a APB out on him.

An hour later he pulled up on Fayette Street in Highlandtown, looking for Azarah's Audi. It was nowhere to be found, so he parked in front of her house, and sparked a blunt. He had run through four blunts, all his weed, Madd Lou's mixtape, and Nyse's mixtape, before Azarah pulled up.

It was ten pm when she pulled up and got out the car. He got out the truck. She spotted him immediately. No more all black clothes, no more hoodies, no more dark shades. He was dressed like the 4Hunnid she first met.

"You not still mad at me, are you?"

"What are you doing here? Do you know what's going on?" she asked.

"Yeah, I know."

"Then you know they could be watching my house for you."

The second the words left her mouth, unmarked and marked police cars stormed the block.

"It was worth it," he smiled, showing off his flawless smile.

"Do you have a gun on you?"

"No. I know what's up."

"Davenport! Get your hands up over your head." They heard Erk yell behind them.

"You still mad?"

"No, I'm not."

"I'm gonna let them give you everything in my pocket. Go to the house and get that bag of stuff I bought you."

"King, none of that is important. They are tryna slam you for these murders," she said, worried.

"Last chance Davenport! Hands up, or we'll do this the hard way!"

"Go get the bag," 4Hunnid said, and turned around to face the polices. "And how much better was the hard way for you the last time you put your hands on me, Erk?" He walked out in the street. "Which one of these cars y'all want me in?" he asked, purposely walking away from Erk.

The officer he walked to, grabbed him and put the cuffs on him. He pulled out the contents of his pockets and placed it on the hood of the car.

"I'll take his belongings," Azarah said.

"You want her to have it?"

"Yeah, give it to her."

"I'll be waiting on you, bae," she said. "I'll call Connie Y too."

"Do that."

***

Central District Police Station...

The Police congratulated Erk on a job well done, when he marched 4Hunnid inside the building. Erk was just as baffled as 4Hunnid, as to why they were clapping. He sat 4Hunnid inside of the interrogation room and left out to find his boss. He found his partners on the tenth floor, sitting outside of the captain's office.

"What's up guys?"

"Jarvos," Coppola said, "where have you been?"

"Picking up our last suspect."

"4Hundred! You got him?"

"Sure did. He's down on the third floor."

"That's why Buetelli is having a meeting with the captain," Travoski said.

"Is that right," he said, and walked into the office.

"Don't..." Coppola was saying before he closed the door behind him.

"Excuse me, were you called in here, officer?"

"No, ma'am. I need to see Lieutenant Buetelli."

(Chuckling) "Do you have any notion as to who office this is?"

He took a deep breath. "I know where I am, secretary. I have some impor—"

"I'm not sure you know, sir. The captain has a policy and she's very strict on that policy being followed. Now, if you want to keep your Job, I'd advise you to—" she was saying before the captain's door opened.

"Courtney, is everything okay?"

"Yes, ma'am. I was just instructing this officer on policy."

Ernie "Erk" Jarvos pulled out his gun and fired four shots into the secretary's face. He turned to the captain and fired six shots in her open mouth.

"Are you okay, Detective Jarvos," the captain asked, snapping him out of his stupor. He shook it off and focused on the woman in front of him.

"Yes, I'm fine."

"Why are you here, detective?"

"I need to see Lieutenant Buetelli."

"And this couldn't wait?"

"I didn't think it could wait. I was certain that he'd want this intel ASAP, Capt'."

"Let me be the judge of that and I hope it's good... your job depends on it."

He was taken aback by her brashness and momentarily stunned into silence.

"I'm listening, detective."

"Oh. I have King Tremaine Davenport, aka 4Hundred, down on the third floor."

"Oh dear. I was looking forward to firing you too. But, if you decide, again, to disregard my office policy, which I'm sure you know; you'll be home without a job. I'm not Buetelli, nor do I have a soft spot for Coppola; you'll be out of here. Now go wait for my instructions on the third floor."

***

Lexington Terrace (New Houses)...
Nyse and DY was sitting in a stolen Dodge Caravan watching a house.

"You sure he in there, DY?"

"Ya dumb-ass boy, I told you the bitch Nikki said this where he been hiding out, since his boys got the axe."

"He better be, or I'm killin' Nikki too."

"So what we gon' sit here, and wait for him to come out?" DY asked.

"Fuck I look like; the police? I ain't sittin' in covert. I'm knockin' on the fuckin' door. Come on."

DY shook his head, grabbed his gun, and got out the van.

"I got this Nyse. Let me handle the door. You said you wanted to torture him, right?"

"Yeah."

"Aiight, let me handle the door."

Nyse sighed. "Go'head boy. You better not fuck this up."

They approached the door. DY motioned for Nyse to stand to the side. He knocked. After two minutes, he knocked again.

"Bitch, I know you in there. What'chu got ah nigga in there?" DY said, and beat on the door. "Carmen! Bitch!"

The door swung open. Rick Flare appeared with a gun in his hand.

"Get lost lil' nigga. Carmen ain't here," he said, to the familiar face.

"What if I 'on't wanna leave? Then what? What are you gonna do next?" DY asked.

"You testing me boy," he said, coming out the door.

Nyse stepped closer and placed both of his guns to Rick Flare's head. That's when it hit him where he knew DY from.

"Drop it, stupid."

Before he had the opportunity to drop it, DY struck him across his face with the .40 he was carrying. Rick Flare fell to the porch floor. The gun fell down the steps.

"Get'cha dumb-ass up, and get the fuck in the house," Nyse said, forcefully.

DY hurriedly grabbed the gun and went in the house.

"See if you can find some tape and put'cha gloves on." Nyse said. He walked behind Rick Flare and put him in the 'L'. He tightened his grip until Rick Flare lost consciousness.

When Rick Flare gained consciousness back he was taped to a chair, pushed up to the kitchen table. Nyse was on one side and DY was on the other side. If it wasn't for him being taped to the chair, it would've looked like they were about to have dinner.

"Let's make a phone call Rick Flare."

"Fuck you, Nyse. You sick bitch."

(Laughing) "Oh, you think I'm playing?"

"Just kill me and get it over with."

"It don't work like that. You see, I made a very special lady a promise, and I want to keep my promise to her. Now, again, I want to make a phone call."

"Make it then!"

"I need the number."

"It's in there under "Bitch"."

He scrolled down on his touch screen Boost Mobile, pressed a button, then put the phone on speaker. No one answered. It took four tries before she answered.

"Let me guess, your boys are dead, you're next, you're scared, and you need some money to disappear," his mother asked.

"Fuck you! I don't need shit from you."

"Hey Ms. Mary. He called because of me."

"And who are you?"

"The guy of your dreams."

"Excuse me."

"The last time I saw you, I made you a promise, and I'm calling to let you hear that I am a man of my word."

"Oh, I know who this is. The young boy with the pipe-laying skills."

"That's me," Nyse smiled and licked his lips.

"Can you come over, once you done there?"

"Freak bitch!"

Nyse punched him in his jaw.

"That sounded like it hurt son, did it?"

"You going to hell!"

"Maybe so, but not before you."

Mary stayed on the phone the whole hour and fifteen minutes it took to kill him.

"You stopping through youngster?"

"You think I'm crazy?"

"Trust me baby, you have absolutely nothing to worry about. Come give me some of that good dick."

DY and Nyse laughed.

"I'll be over, but I'm wearing the ski-mask, and I'm bringing two big-ass guns, with two extended clips."

"So long as the dick with you, I wouldn't care what else you bring."

"Aiight, I warned you."

"See you soon," she said, and hung up.

"You better not go over that bitch house."

"I ain't stupid, Yummy. I ain't going over there."

DY knew he was lying, but he let it go for the sake of argument.

CHAPTER 24
Breaking News

Central Police Station...
Interrogation Room #306

4Hunnid hadn't ate or slept since they brought him in the day before. It was going on seventeen hours since they had him, and not one person came to see him. Although this was the longest he had ever sat without being charged, he still wasn't worried. They had to charge him or release him in twenty-four hours. That he knew for sure.

On the eighteenth hour, someone threw a brown bag and a bottle of water through the slot on the door. He grabbed the bag, opened it and frowned. There were two hard slices of bread and a packet of peanut butter. He hated peanut butter. He threw the bag against the wall and picked up the bottle. The water had a little bit more sizzle to it than it should've been when he shook it up. But the absolute deal breaker, on the water, was that the seal had already been broken on it. He threw that against the wall as well.

Twenty minutes later Coppola and Jarvos walked in the room, with folders in their hand, and took a seat. 4Hunnid smirked at them.

"4Hunnid, what's mobbin' Piru?"

"Wrong hood, Erk. You know what the fuck I am."

"Go'head and get rowdy. I want you to, so I can literally beat the shit out of you. I still owe you from the radio station stunt you pulled."

"You still can't fuck with me. My hands like that."

"Can we get to it?" Coppola asked.

"Coppola, you know damn well I'm not answering shit without my lawyer. Where is she?"

"She's wrapped up right now. In the moan time, what can you tell me about the murders of the Slaughtermore artists?"

"The only thing I can tell you is you phat as shit Coppola and you look like you got some good pussy."

She was appalled by his answer. He smiled.

Erk stood up and grabbed him by his YSL jacket. 4Hunnid pushed his hands away from him, and jumped up in a fighting stance. He was ready now.

"You know the saying Erk, put'cha hands on someone, they put'em back on you."

"Sit down Davenport. Jarvos, sit and keep your hands to yourself."

Erk sat down and so did 4Hunnid.

"Yo, I ain't answering shit, until my lawyer get here. So until then, we can sit and talk about how I think that you have silky pussy hairs and—"

"Enough disrespect. Davenport!"

"No! The disrespect is you bringing me in here, without my lawyer, thinkin' umma say anything! You ma'fuckas know what it is! I ain't saying shit!"

Jerkman Travoski walked in the room, and whispered in Erk's ear.

"What?!"

He started whispering again.

"Shit!"

Jerk left out, leaving Erk fuming mad. The vain in his forehead was evidence enough.

"Do you need to step out, Jarvos?" Coppola asked.

"We both need to," he said, and stood up.

"In the middle—"

"Come on, Coppola."

They both stepped out. Jerk was standing there with Lieutenant Buetelli, and their captain; Captain Bria Glockfernelli.

"What's wrong?" Coppola asked.

"A few things," Buetelli said. "The main thing is Fredrick Caldon, Gerald Evergreen, and Travis McMeekins were found brutally murdered in various parts of the city."

"What?!" Coppola exclaimed. "Fry, Rick Flare, and Fox."

"This is not good."

"I'd say," Jarvos said. "We have the whole Toe Taggin' in custody and have had them in custody for over twenty-four hours. What was the time of death."

"It wasn't them," the captain said. "Get this shit over and get them out of my building. While you're wasting time interrogating these people, you could've been in the streets saving those three lives that was lost last night. Stop fucking around. They're already talking about pulling funding on this unit. We need results."

"We're on it Capt'."

"Don't give us that shit, Jarvos. You're lucky your ass still have your badge. Cut them loose. Now."

"Yes, sir."

The captain left with Buetelli on her heels.

"Travoski, you and Coppola release everyone. I'll handle Davenport." They gave him the look. "I got him. Relax."

"It's your badge," Coppola said.

He walked back inside the room by himself. 4Hunnid jumped up in a fighter stance.

"Sit the fuck down. I'm not gonna fuck you up. I came back to present you with a once in a lifetime opportunity. Sit."

"I thought you ma'fuckas was tired of playin' games?"

"I am. That's why I'm laying it all on the table. Take a seat."

4Hunnid still stood.

"Please," Erk said.

4Hunnid saw that it hurt him to say please. He laughed and sat down.

"What the fuck you want cop?"

(Sighing) "Look, I hate your guts. That's no secret, but you are highly intelligent. You're no dummy."

(Laughing) "So you want me to tell on somebody or something, so I can go on living life as a snitch-ass-bitch. No thank you, I love being gangsta. Everything about me is on the up and up. I ain't no fuck-boy."

(Laughing) "You really think you have it all figured out? Well, you don't. You and your crew is so close to going to the penitentiary that I'm surprised you all don't smell the commissary already," he said. "Last chance Davenport. Before you answer, know that we have a confidential informant inside your circle already. We got enough to snatch you now, but we're just waiting for the icing on the cake."

"Fuck you Erk! Fuck you think you talking to? I don't believe shit you say pig, and even if you did have one, fuck'em. Just remember every action has a reaction. We all must pay for our sins in the end. Now let me the fuck go."

"The door is right there, but you remember this: time tells you everything you need to know about a person."

"Yeah, fuck you," 4Hunnid said, and walked out.

***

Everyone got released and left alone. Toe Taggin' Pose Music Group went back to making music with strict orders from Jerrod, to not mention any member of Slaughtermore or about their murders. There was a lot of speculations surrounding the murders, but no one knew for sure.

4Hunnid went back into reclusion to make things right with Azarah. She was still pissed off at him and he wanted to show her that he was serious about being in a relationship with her. She had to teach him, because he really didn't know how to be in one. At the same time, Azarah was pressing him to get back on the hip hop scene.

His whereabouts was still a hot topic. He wasn't budging though. He promised her he'd get back on the scene after the Pier 6 concert. He said he'd be a fan this go around and he'd be in the next big show they had. No one liked his decision, but they understood and loved him, so they supported him. They still had yet to physically lay eyes on him.

Magik, Madd Lou, Wild Bill, L-Trigga, Nyse, and DY went back to selling dope. Samantha and Looney Redz went on recording music. The CEO of Slaughtermore Records, Spider, recruited some more young boys to carry on the torch. These young boys were more so savages than rappers. They could rap, so Spider figured he would build off of that.

***

(May 10, 2014) Weeks later
Pier 6 Concert Pavilion…
Thomas Gruden walked in their dressing room with Tammy Gruden on his ass; both of them looking and smelling like straight cash money.

"Congratulations, Jerrod. You pulled it off. You managed to sell out the Pavilion. Every chair is filled and the lawn cannot be seen."

"I told you we would."

"I put my money where my mouth was. I've even decided to add an extra five thousand to everyone's check."

"That's fine."

"You don't seem excited Jerrod. What's wrong?"

"This is 'excited' for Jerrod, Mr. Gruden," Amil said. "Anything else and you'd be asking for too much."

"Okay, well, congrats again. I can't wait to see the show," Tom said, and left.

Amil walked over to Jerrod. "What's wrong Jerrod, and don't tell me nothing?"

"That shit don't feel right Amil. At all."

"What do you mean?"

"4Hunnid ain't here. Something else is going on with him. When have he ever turned down an audience? This is what he lives for. That boy has skills that capture the hearts and minds of everyone looking. He loves the attraction of the crowd. Did you watch the footage from the Baltimore Arena show?"

"I did."

"You probably though he was high as ah kite on there."

"He was," she said.

"Wrong. He was sober, period. No drugs or alcohol was in him. He performed the show naturally. I just don't get why he gave it up. This ain't him."

"We'll worry about that later. Right now, we got a show to do. We gotta go with what we have Jerrod."

Magik and Madd Lou walked in the room.

"I 'on't know how y'all pulled this shit off, with the homie being the host, but that's what's poppin'," Magik said, excitedly.

"The homegirl Lady Red made it happen. We gon' bring the house down tonight. Get everyone in here."

"Aiight," Magik said, and left.

"Madd Lou you ready?"

"I was born ready, Amil."

Ten minutes later the whole gang was together and standing in a circle.

"Each one of us is living out our dreams. I want you all to look at this moment as a blessing. Enjoy the moment. Have fun."

The stage director came in.

"Excuse me. In ten minutes, we will be ready for the first act."

"Aiight," Wild Bill said. "You up Nyse."

"I'm ready to go out here and kill this shit."

"You better nigga," Amil said.

The lights went off inside of Pier 6. The crowd went crazy. When the lights came back on, Nyse was standing in the middle of the stage with his shirt off. The females began yelling his name and 'I Love Yous'.

"If you fuckin' wit' me tonight put'cha motherfuckin' diamonds in the air!" Nyse finally said. The crowd reacted immediately.

"Carey Street!" the crowd chanted.

Nyse smiled and looked back at his DJ. "You heard'em Chase, drop the motherfuckin' beat."

The *Carey Street* beat dropped and Nyse went crazy.

He performed like his life depended on it. Almost every song the crowd yelled out, he performed. *Grown Man Bars*, *Domiēr*, *Wild Niggas, and Two Glock 40s*. The crowd was screaming for *Illuminati*, but he threw up the diamond sign with his hands and left the stage.

"Baltimore! Make some motherfuckin' noise for the first lady of Toe Taggin' Posse Music Group; Queen Azarahhhh!" DJ Flee yelled, from behind the DJ's table.

Azarah walked out on the stage to a standing ovation.

She blew kisses, and waved at the audience.

"Hey Baltimore!" The crowd went crazy. "Let me talk to my ladies real quick. Where my ladies that like to dress sexy for their man?" The ladies began screaming. "Well, you gonna love this. It's the second single off my highly-anticipated album; Queen of Diamonds. It's called Balenciaga Panties!"

She began singing; stealing the show with her amazing voice. She held the audience's attention for twenty minutes, singing her captivating songs like, *Red Bottom Bandit*, *Eat Me 2 Sleep*, *Loving A G*, *Faithful*, and she ended her set with *Shaky Love*.

Train was next to come out. He warmed the crowd up with *Tricks On You*, *Watch Me*, *Thinking Slow*, and *Train Smoke*.

As soon as Train left the stage a burgundy Chevy 64 pulled up on the stage. When it stopped, the switches was hit, and the car door opened. A guy got out with a burgundy lumberjack on, a pair of khaki shorts and a pair of burgundy Chuck Taylors.

"It's YG 4 Hunniiiiiiiiiid!" the Compton Tree Top Piru rapper yelled on the mic. "I'm here tonight for my homies! Y'all supported them, so I'm introducin' them! Without further ado, introducing my motherfuckin' brothers! Toe! Taggin'! Posse!"

It got dark again. YG hopped in the car and drove off the stage.

"We here!" the Trojan Boyz ran on the stage with fake assault weapons.

"Is this ah motherfuckin' party or what?" Wild Bill asked.

The crowd yelled back.

"You sure? This ma'fucka feels incomplete! Like something's missing," Wild Bill said.

"Where the blunts of that loud pack at?!" Madd Lou asked.

The crowd roared.

"I 'on't smell shit! Light it up!"

"I 'on't know Lou. This shit still feel incomplete."

The crowd went crazy when Magik walked out on the stage with a weapon similar to the Trojan Boyz' weapons.

"Okay, here I go, lets get this ma'fucka started!"

The crowd began chants of 4Hunnid. The beat dropped and Wild Bill performed *Gunz In My Hand*, *On My Best Bullshit*, *Head Shots*, and *Dead Rat* with ab-lib help from his brothers. Madd Lou took over next, performing *5 Feet Assassin*, *Army Gunz*, *Trial & Error*, *Dope Dealers*, and *Fuck Yo Hood*.

Magik stepped to the front of the stage and looked out at the sea of people.

"I 'on't think this bitch loud enough. What'chall think?"

The rest of them stepped up to the front of the stage.

"Naw Magik, this bitch definitely not loud enough," Wild Bill said, cupping his free hand behind his ear.

DJ Flee dropped the beat to *Mr. Zero To 4Hunnid* and the whole Pier 6 shook. The Toe Taggin' members looked at Flee. He was specifically told not to put none of 4Hunnid's music on the laptop, so mistakes like this wouldn't happen. The crowd was so loud, they couldn't even hear themselves think. DJ Flee just shrugged his shoulders apologetically.

"I know y'all ain't think this would be a motherfuckin' party without ya boy 4Hunniiiid!"

Everybody began looking around. 4Hunnid ran on the stage, causing the whole Pier 6 to erupt in noise. He smiled and hugged his brothers. He was at home in this atmosphere. This is what he missed.

Magik performed all new songs and wasn't surprised at all that 4Hunnid knew every one of them. The first song was *TC*; *Tasty Candidate*, *Hand Signs*, *My Shoes 2 Hunnid*, *Dress Code*, *Go to War*, and *Done Did It Already*.

4Hunnid closed the show with doing the songs that he had with each member of Toe Taggin' Posse. He even brung Azarah back out and did the remixes to her songs. He performed five new songs of his own too; *THOTS*, *Forever TTP*, *Loyalty*, *I Can't Be Broken* and *Unwilling*.

"Come on out here relative!" 4Hunnid said, on the mic.

L-Trigga walked out on the stage.

"This right here is the hardest working nigga I know. Y'all know him. He's behind the best parties in the city. You wanna throw ah party in the city, make sure it got that Kode of Silence ENT seal on it. I love you relative." 4Hunnid said. "I wanna address one more thing before we go. Y'all already know what it is with me. I'm forever Toe Taggin' Posse! Nyse! Come on out here, and show'em how tight we is."

The *Illuminati* beat dropped and the crowd went crazy.

Everyone on the stage grabbed up the assault weapons, pointed them at the crowd and pulled the triggers. Foam shot from the guns and at the same time fell from the ceiling of the pavilion. The crowd sung every bar of the popular song with them without missing a word. The show ended with Azarah pulling 4Hunnid off the stage playfully.

"Great show guys," Thomas Gruden said, excitedly. "You guys fuckin' ripped it."

"Oh shit, the cops," Nyse said, and took off like a bat out of hell.

He said it so fast and ran even faster, that no one had a chance to process what he said, until it was too late, and they were surrounded by police officers.

"Jerrod Frampton, Arlando Gilyard (Magik), King Davenport, Louis Ramsey (Madd Lou), Damon Owens (Wild Bill), Katrina Clayborne, Steven Johnson (L-Trigga), Trayvon Cox (Dummy Yummy), Deyonté Harvey (Nyse), and Amil DeCario; you are all under arrest. You have a right to remain silent. Anything you say, can and will be used against you in the court of law. You have a right to an attorney. If you don't have one, one will be appointed to you…"

They were all arrested and transported to Central Bookings Intake Facility, located on Madison Street. Their warrant papers read like this:

State of Maryland V. Jerrod Frampton

1. **Jerrod Frampton:** *Distribution of heroin, Kingpin Stature, Conspiracy*

2. **Arlando Gilyard:** *Distribution of heroin, Conspiracy to distribute heroin, Possession of stolen firearm*

3. **King Davenport:** *Distribution of heroin, Conspiracy to distribute heroin, Possession of stolen firearm, 1st Degree Murder, 1st Degree Assault on a police officer, Deadly Weapon w/ intent to injure*

4. **Louis Ramsey:** *Distribution of heroin, 1st Degree Murder, Possession of deadly weapons, Conspiracy*

5. **Damon Owens**: *Distribution of heroin, 1st Degree Murder, Conspiracy*

6. **Steven Johnson:** *Distribution of heroin, Conspiracy*

7. **Trayvon Cox:** *Distribution of heroin, Conspiracy*

8. **Deyonté Harvey:** *Distribution of heroin, 1st Degree Murder, Rape, Home Invasion, 1st Degree Assault, Conspiracy*

9. **Katrina Clayborne:** *Conspiracy to distribute heroin, Conspiracy*

10. **Amil DeCario:** *Money Laundering, Fraud, Conspiracy*

***

Connie Y's house...

She was enjoying her Saturday night; something she hadn't been able to do in a minute. She had her nephew's mixtape playing real loud on her surround sound while she prepared a chicken salad for a late-night snack.

She took her food to her room, cut the TV on, grabbed a file on a murder case she was working on, and sat indian-style on her queen size bed. On her fourth fork of salad her house phone rung. She leaned over towards the phone to see her secretary's name pop up. She sighed and picked up the phone. She could barely hear Teresa, because it was so much noise in the background.

"Hello," Connie said. Teresa began talking real fast.

The noise only made it worst. Connie couldn't understand anything she was saying. "Call me when you get somewhere quiet, because I can't hear you," she said, and hung up. She figured Teresa was calling her to tell her how good the show was.

Connie went back to her salad and murder case. She was so engulfed in the case that she didn't see her nephew and his friends' faces pop up on her TV screen. The Breaking News news cast was lost on her; but was so close.

Twenty minutes later her phone rung once again. She leaned over this time to a number she didn't recognize. She ignored the phone and went back to the task at hand. She looked over at her empty water glass.

"Shoot," she fussed, grabbing the glass.

As she was walking down the steps, she thought, *why was anyone calling her house phone.* The water was temporarily forgotten and she began her cell phone hunt. She found the iPhone, she used for her clients only, on the charger by the knives. It took her ten minutes to find her regular iPhone in her Gucci bag. She was shocked to see that she had sixty missed calls.

"Oh Jesus. What now," she said to herself, as she clicked on the number she saw the most.

The woman picked up immediately.

"I've been calling you all night."

"What's wrong, Azarah?"

"Everybody got locked up at the show earlier tonight."

"What?" she exclaimed. "Everybody like who?"

"Everybody, like everybody. Jerrod, Madd Lou, Wild Bill, Amil, Magik, L-Trigga, Trina, DY, and your nephew."

"I thought he wasn't performing tonight?"

"Well, he did, and brung the house down too. Right after the show, the police bumrushed us backstage, and started slapping cuffs on people. They had a warrant for Nyse too, but he hauled ass when he spotted the police."

"What about Tommy, Flee, Taedo, Train, Sos'a, and Dee Dee?"

"We were all there. They didn't even bat an eye at us," Azarah said.

"There's nothing we can do now. It's Saturday. They won't go for bail review until Monday. The only thing we can do is wait until they call us. Where are you?"

"I'm at the store with Dee Dee. They are searching if from top to bottom."

"Are they destroying the store?"

"No. Dee Dee let them know that the whole store was wired with video and audio."

"That was smart of her. I need you to be smart as well. An indictment of this magnitude doesn't just stop here. It actually begins at the arrest. They will monitor every phone call they make over there. Don't expect too many calls. Their 'no phone' policy goes for in jail too; especially jail. The visits too, but don't talk about the case or anything illegal while on the visit. All other business will come through me. Our conversations can't be monitored."

"This shit is crazy."

"We'll see what the charges are tomorrow. Go home and get some sleep. Also, are you gonna be staying at the house?"

"I haven't made up my mind yet."

"Yet? You know the same rules apply for that house, right?"

"I know Connie. I'll watch myself, if I go there."

"Okay," she said. "See you tomorrow." As soon as she hung up, she looked up and saw the news. Ten faces were on the screen with Breaking News over top of the mug shots.

CHAPTER 25
Letters of Intent

Looney Redz' House...

Samantha was singing in the kitchen, cooking dinner for her depressed boyfriend. Looney Redz life had done a three hundred and sixty degree turn. One minute he was rapping, getting money, and doing big things with his friends. The next minute, all of his friends are dead, he has a new rap team, he has a new production team, and he was right back at the bottom, broke and still in debt with his connect. The worst part of all, he lost his brother. He was sick behind losing him, but was glad they were able to reconcile their differences before he passed away. The only good thing to come out of this catastrophe, in his eyes, was that the Toe Taggin' Posse Music Group was going to finally get what they deserve.

He had lost his passion for music and rarely, if ever, went to their studio. When he did pop in, he was sure to find The Savages; the new recruits to Slaughtermore Records. He walked in on a session they were having one day and was impressed by what he heard; but they weren't his crew, and The Savages popped every pill imaginable; oxycodone, amphetamine, diazepam, Percocet etc etc. They were too much like dope fiends for him to hang with. He did the music he was contracted to do, and got missing, and Samantha was never allowed to be around them.

"The food ready, daddy," Samantha cooed.

He got up off the couch and went to the kitchen. Ten minutes into his meal someone rung his house bell.

"I'll get it."

"Put some clothes on first," he said.

She went upstairs, threw on a pair of pajama pants, a bra, and a tank top and went to answer the door.

"Heeyyy," she said, opening the door.

"What's up Sam? How is he?"

"I got him eating now, but he's still having problems sleeping. He's doing better."

"Good. I don't have to come in here and force feed him," Lisa said, hugging Samantha. She walked in the kitchen and saw her brother looking better than he had been in weeks. "You looking good baby bro'."

He looked up from his plate. "Hey Lisa. What's up?"

"You tell me. How you feeling?"

"Better."

"Good, because daddy sent me over here to check on you and to also tell you the police stopped pass the house."

Ding! Ding! Ding! The doorbell chimed.

"Go see who the fuck that is, Sam. What did the police want?"

"They were asking questions about Traum. They asked daddy about some rap beef. They also asked—" she was saying before she was silenced by Samantha and two plain-clothed cops.

"Fuck is y'all doing in my house?" Looney Redz jumped up from his chair.

"Calm down Mr. Weathers. We're here to help."

"Cut the bullshit, Coppola. Help what? Get the fuck outta here! Sam, show'em the door."

"So you're gonna let them get away with killing your brother?" Travoski asked, sliding Traum's crime scene photos across the kitchen table.

"That shit ain't gon' work on me, Jerk. Do y'all jobs. I'm not gon' do it for you."

"Evergreen was helping us before he was killed."

"Bullshit!"

"Oh really," Travoski said. "How do you think we knew about his mother being raped by Deyonté Harvey?"

"I 'on't know shit about that."

"We can put these guys away forever," Coppola said, a little bit too desperately. "You can help us do that, and you can become what you once were."

"Get the fuck out!"

Lisa was eye-hustling the papers in Coppola's hand when something caught her eye.

"What is it exactly, are you asking from my brother?"

"We need some details on the beef between Slaughtermore and Toe Taggin' Posse."

"And who is Toe Taggin' Posse?"

"These guys," Coppola said, laying the mug shots on the table.

She almost fainted when she saw the picture of 4Hunnid. She played it off by sitting down at the kithen table. She picked up 4Hunnid's picture. All eyes went on her.

"Do you know him?" Coppola asked.

She thought about it for a moment. "I saw him out front, two days before my brother was killed."

Coppola and Travoski's eyes glittered with hope. Placing 4Hunnid at the scene, even if it was two days before, was a big break in their case.

"Are you sure you seen this man out front?" Coppola asked

"Don't say no more, Lisa," Looney Redz warned.

"Yes, I'm sure," she said, ignoring him. "He was lost and asked me where Southgreen Road was. He told me his name was KT. I told him my name was Lisa," she said, and started crying, as she remembered the fellatio she gave 4Hunnid.

"You mind giving us a statement?" Jerkman asked.

"Leave her alone and get the fuck out!"

"Y'all need to leave now," Samantha said.

"You wanna go to jail for obstruction?" Jerkman asked. "Sit down and shut the fuck up."

Coppola consoled Lisa Weathers until she got herself together. They got her statement once she calmed down and it went like this:

"I was coming out the house, ready to get in my car when I saw him looking at a piece of paper, and up the street like he was lost. I walked over to him, introduced myself and asked him was he lost. He told me his name was KT and showed me a piece of paper with the street he was looking for. I told him it was four blocks over and that was it. I walked away."

"Did you see him again?"

"No."

"What about on the day Lawrence was killed? You got a good look at the assailant, right?"

"I did," she said, thinking back. She looked at the photos on the table to see if one of the guys could fit the description of who she saw. None of them seemed to fit the husky assailant she seen. "I don't believe it was KT. The guy I seen was a bit husky. Too big to be KT. KT was muscular."

"I thank you for your cooperation. It shows you really cared for Lawrence," Coppola said.

Lisa started crying again.

***

Detective Ernie 'Erk' Jarvos stood back as Detective Che Molino knocked on the door.

A woman came to the door. "Yes, may I help you?"

"Yes. I'm Detective Molino and this is Detective Jarvos. We'd like to talk to you about your son. Can we come in?"

She hesitated at first, but then let them in. "Can I get you two something to drink."

"No, ma'am."

"I'm fine."

They all sat down in the living room. She tied her robe up nice and tight. She didn't want them to see that she was naked underneath.

"Ma'am, you may or may not be aware, but your son was working with us before he was killed." She looked disgusted, but Molino continued. "He told us that you were raped by a rival rapper of his. I'm curious as to why you never reported the sexual assault."

"Because it never happened. I loved my son dearly, and I'm still hurting over the lost, but my son was a compulsive liar. He would lie, even when he didn't have to. That was Gerald. Just like his daddy."

"So you're saying no one came in here, tied you up, demanded that you call your son so he could be lead to his death, but refused to come, so one guy raped you?"

"No, that never happened. If someone raped me, I would've called the police," she said.

"Gerald also told us that you were angry about him not taking your spot with the kidnappers, and that one of the kidnappers promised you that he'd make sure Gerald suffered a horrible death for his cowardness. Is there any truth to that?"

With a straight face, she said, "No, there isn't. I told you my son was a compulsive liar."

"When was the last time you spoke to your son, Ms. Hanson?"

"On the night he died," she smartly said.

"For how long?"

"Thirty minutes, I don't know. I can't remember. That was a month ago."

"Records show that you were on the phone with him for one hour and fifteen minutes," Molino said.

"That's your answer then. I said I didn't remember."

"Do you recall what you two talked about?"

"Me and my son didn't have the best relationship. He must've felt the end near because he called me to pour his heart out. He apologized for everything for the most part."

"Did you hear anyone in the background?"

"No."

"Did he tell you where he was?"

"No."

They all heard someone coming down the steps. Her friend stood at the bottom of the steps in nothing but his boxer briefs, scratching his sack, with his eyes almost closed.

"I'm high as ah bitch," he giggled. "Mary! Where you at girl?!"

Molino and Jarvos looked at one another in shock. Both officers jumped up and pulled out their guns.

"Put your hands up!" Molino yelled.

He was so high, he couldn't do nothing but continue to scratch his sack and smile.

"What are y'all doing?!" Mary asked.

"Back the fuck up before you go to jail for harboring a fugitive."

"Fugitive?"

"He's a suspect on the Illuminati indictment."

"And the same man that's charged with your son's murder."

"Deyonté Harvey, you are under arrest. You have the right…"

Nyse eyes opened wide, finally processing what was going on. "Erk? Was'sup wit'cha dumbass boy?"

Molino put the cuffs on Nyse while Jarvos read him his rights.

"You all got the wrong man. This is my friend."

"Ms. Hanson, we have the right guy," he said.

"Molino, I'll finish the interview, you put Harvey in the car."

"I beg your pardon. This is my interview. You take him to the car, and I'll finish the interview."

Jarvos knew he was skating on thin ice, so he took Molino's advice. When he left, Molino continued the interview.

"What is your relationship to Mr. Harvey, Ms. Hanson?"

"My friend."

"Friend, huh? How old are you Ms. Hanson?"

"Fifty-four going on twenty-four."

"Harvey is twenty-three."

"Well, I guess that makes me one year older than him," she laughed.

Molino shook his head. "Did your son know about your relationship with Mr. Harvey?"

"Yes and we argued about it."

"How did you meet him?"

"At a concert. I don't remember which one. I know it was about six months ago. We were talking, the next thing I know, we were dancing, and the next, in a hotel room bed. He gives me the greatest sex." She said, running her hands over her breast.

"Excuse me Ms. Hanson, can you stay on track? So you believe your son told us that story about you getting raped by Harvey, because he was angry over you two's relationship?"

"I don't believe my son told you all anything, but if he did, I can only imagine so. No one knows what was going through the head of my son. Have you ever sat and listened to his raps? They're dark."

"I find it hard to believe that Gerald would lie to us."

"And that's whose problem? Certainly, not mine. Look, I've answered all of your questions. Is it against the law to jump on a dick that's thirty-one years younger than you?"

"No, ma'am."

"Then I've broken no laws. I would like for you to leave now."

Detective Molino stood up. "I'll be in touch, Ms. Hanson."

"Have a good day."

***

Baltimore City Detention Center (aka Steel Side)...

The men on the case was was denied bond and was transported to Steel Side to await trial. Trina was released on a two hundred and fifty-thousand-dollar bail. Amil was released on a hundred-thousand-dollar bail. Every person on the case had a paid notable attorney. Connie couldn't represent them all, but she was appointed the lead attorney on the case and of course she represented her nephew.

Because of the ongoing war between the Bloods and the BGF inside of Steel Side, the administration wanted to put Jerrod, Magik, Wild Bill, Madd Lou, L-Trigga, and 4Hunnid on "F" section or "G" section, which was where all of the Bloods and Pirus was housed at, but they weren't having it; none of them. They forced them to place them on other sections. They had to sign off on it, but whatever it took to not be placed on "F" or "G" sections. 85% of the jail was BGF, but that concerned them none. Dummy Yummy didn't have a problem being placed, because of his BGF ties.

4Hunnid and Madd Lou was placed on "N" section. Jerrod went on "Q" section. Wild Bill and Magik was placed on "S" section. Dummy Yummy and L-Trigga was placed on "O" section. Their first two weeks was regular over there. After two weeks, the COs rolled

111

out the red carpet for them. They were either fans or groupies. They carried themselves as men, so the other inmates carried them as men.

Today, they had pulled some strings so that they all could meet up in the jail's library. They badly needed to piece together a plan and not solely rely on the lawyers.

4Hunnid was the last one to enter the library. Everyone was sitting at one table talking. Before he said one word, he checked under the chairs and tables in the library, looking for bugs or wires or any other listening device.

"I don't trust this shit my niggas," 4Hunnid said.

"Me either, but we need this meeting," Jerrod countered.

"So what's the plan?" Madd Lou asked.

"From what I know from Kia (his lawyer), they got some witnesses that'll testify that they bought dope from 4Hunnid, Magik, Madd Lou, and Dummy Yummy. They hit all of y'all stash houses and found shit," Jerrod said, pulling a piece of paper from his pocket.

"4Hunnid and Magik, they found vacuum sealed items, two digital scales and a bunch of baggies. No money, no guns, and no drugs; not even residue. Madd Lou and Wild Bill, they hit five houses in the projects in y'all's name. All together they found twenty hollow point bullets, a shotgun, an ounce of weed, and a voice modulator. Dummy Yummy, they found two packages of cocaine in your stash house. One was nine hundred eighty point one grams and the other one was six hundred forty-two point eight grams. They also found one hundred sixty-two thousand, five hundred and thirty-two dollars in the wall."

"Damn, they found my young nigga stash spot," Dummy Yummy smiled.

"In my house, they claim they found six kilograms of pure heroin, seven loaded handguns, an AR-15 assault rifle, seven hundred thousand dollars in uncashed bank checks, two hundred thousand, seven hundred and sixty dollars in cash, ten ounces of weed and a ledger that they claim holds all of the names of the people I was serving and what they owed."

All eyes went to Jerrod.

"What? I hope y'all don't think I'm stupid. These ma'fuckas are lying. I never write shit down. They lying about the work too. Six ki's in my house? I've never even took work to my house. Trigga, they hit your stash house and found fiends in there gettin' high, a loaded ACP. 45, two Rugers, some baggies, three ounces of weed, and two masks."

"The good thing we got going for us is they don't have us personally making any sales and the biggest thing; no phone calls between us," Madd Lou said. "I been reading this shit. It's three prongs that gotta be satisfied in order to prove conspiracy. One, they gotta establish that an agreement to possess heroin with intent to distribute the substance existed between two or more persons. Two, the defendant knew of the conspiracy. And three, the defendant knowingly and voluntarily became part of the conspiracy."

"We can beat this shit then?" L-Trigga said.

"What about the ledger? Don't that connect us?" Dummy Yummy asked.

"It does," Wild Bill said.

"I'm tellin' you, there is no ledger. The only thing they could be talking about is the paper I had on my desk with y'all names, and what y'all was being paid to do Pier 6."

"Let's hope that's it."

A CO came in the library. All of them faced her.

"What's up Crystal?" L-Trigga asked.

"I know I said I wouldn't bother y'all, but someone wants to join y'all."

"What?" they all said, simultaneously.

She just shrugged her shoulders.

"This ain't no get together yo. I told you what's up."

"I know Trigga but—"

"Was'sup wit'ch'all dumbasses," Nyse said, walking through the library doors.

They couldn't believe it. Nyse went around dapping everyone up.

"Aiight, Crystal. No more interruptions."

"Okay," she said, and walked away.

"When you get locked up?"

"Last week. They got me on some luck shit. They popped up over Rick Flare's mother's house to question her, and I was over there high-as-ah-bitch, in my draws."

"Fuck was you doing over there?" Jerrod asked.

"Hidin' out over my old head's house."

"I thought you was long gone, Nyse."

"Gone where? Shit, I was right under their nose the whole time I was on the run. If I wasn't so high, I would've still been on the run."

They filled Nyse in on what they was discussing, but it all went in one ear and out the other. His concern was who had the mule, because he was trying to get high.

"You haven't said one word since we been up here, Magik. You aiight?"

"I'm straight Jerrod."

"You sure?"

"Positive. I feel like we in ah uproar for nothing. We good. We gon' have to sit it out, but we gon' beat it? I'm four hunnid percent sure we gon' beat it."

Everyone looked at him strange.

He chuckled. "Everybody relax, this is a vacation. We'll be back out soon. Take this break to sharpen your skills."

Later on...

Madd Lou and 4Hunnid was smoking blunts and writing rhymes in their cell, which was what they did most of the time.

"Lou, you think 2 Hunnid lost his mind bruh?"

"I 'on't know. You saw the look on his face? He was looking like he know for sure we gon' beat this shit."

"Yeah (chuckling), his confidence was high as me..."

They heard the front grill open, so they put the cigarellos out. A female CO showed up in front of their cell.

"4Hunnid, Lou; y'all got something for y'all crazy-ass co-defendant? I hope y'all do, because he is down on "J" section acting up already."

"What is he doing?" 4Hunnid asked.

"He smacked some boy down there who threatened to get him sanctioned by a few comrades. He's just down there acting up."

"Come back in four minutes."

"Okay," she told Madd Lou, and walked off.

He got up, went to his stash, grabbed a 'street-ounce' and threw it on the bed. 4Hunnid pulled a sandwich bag of tabacco from his dip and threw that on the bed next to the weed. Madd Lou pulled a five inch flip out knife from his dip and threw that on the bed along with some cigarellos and a lighter.

4Hunnid wrapped it all in a towel nice and tight. The CO came back ten minutes later, thanked them and rolled out. They went back to smoking.

***

The eight, male co-defendants spent their whole time over Steel Side high. Six months later is when their second wave of motions was mailed to them and this wave caused them to worry; everyone except Magik, who was really treating the stay like a vacation. Wild Bill sent word to them everyday that he was ready to strangle Magik.

The second wave of motions were more detailed and scarier. The other part that was bothering them, was that the state wasn't offereing them any plea bargins, unless cooperation was involved. They were all trying to remain positive and strong, but the stress and uneasiness was beginning to show. They had the weed to take their minds off of reality, but even that wasn't enough sometimes. They were even tired of Magik's positive attitude and his outlook on the entire situation.

Then on the year anniversary of their arrest, 4Hunnid, Madd Lou, Wild Bill, and Nyse received letters in the mail saying that the state intended to seek the death penalty for them. Those letters felt like the nails in their coffins.

***

"S" Section...

The CO walked on the tier and saw Magik playing spades in the dayroom.

"Magik, can you call your cellbuddy? He has to sign for this legal mail."

"Aiight. Yo, hold the hand. I'll be right back. Make sure they don't cheat, Tical."

He got Wild Bill and ran back to the dayroom. He was gambling. The courts, or anything they had to say didn't concern him or worry him in the least. He really didn't care and felt in his mind and heart that he was on vacation. Twenty minutes later he smelled the aroma of the blueberry haze. He told the guys he was taking a brief intermission and jogged back to his cell. He found Wild Bill shaking, smoking the fattest blunt he'd ever saw.

"What's up bruh?"

Wild Bill didn't answer him, he just kept on smoking. Magik spotted the opened letter on his bed. He picked it up and read it.

"Mr. Owens, this is a letter informing you that the state intends to seek the death penalty. Damn bruh," he said, and sat the letter down. "These bitches trying their best. Yo, don't trip off this shit. Ain't none of us going to jail. We just playing the waiting game."

"Not now Magik. Don't start that shit."

"I'm dead ass serious, Bill. That's my word, we ain't going to jail."

Wild Bill, tired of Magik's crazy-talk, got up and left out of the cell.

***

"J" Section...

Nyse had a blunt hanging from his lips with one eye closed, to avoid the smoke, as he read the letter he had just signed for.

"Oh shit, they tryna kill me," Nyse let his arms go slack, he leaned his torso back a little bit and started doing Problem's Hyphy Dance. "Straight up!" he yelled. "Death penalty! Straight up!" He laughed hysterically for thirty minutes straight, then smoked himself silly.

***

"N" Section...

"Damn 4Hunnid, these bitches really tryna kill us."

"Yeah," he said, holding on to his letter, "They is, ain't they."

"Even the lawyers sounding defeated."

"Yours too?" 4Hunnid asked. "My lawyer raised me and I know her better than she knows herself. She put on that tough role around me, but I see it in her eyes. We gon' need a fucking miracle lil' bruh."

"Tell me about it."

"I need Magik's confidence right now." 4Hunnid laughed nervously.

CHAPTER 26
Loyal

Toe Taggin' Attire…
…I lay in bed at night, tryna ignore thoughts of you.
It doesn't seem to be working, tell me what do I supposed to do.
How did we end up here, we supposed to be living it up.
Your smile, your kiss, your touch I miss I could never ever get enough…

Azarah sung her heart out on the track she named *KING*. Sos'a had his eyes closed, enthralled in the melody that easily flowed from Azarah's lips, while Taedo pushed and pulled on buttons and levers on the mixing board. Dee Dee looked on from the door with watchful, skeptical eyes. She no longer trusted Azarah.

She had been knowing Jerrod since she was young, so he trusted her with his business and for as long as he's been doing his thing in the streets, he was never careless. He taught those close to him about the carelessness, so with all the evidence the state had, it could have come from only one source; someone close to them. She would jump from a project roof before betraying any one of them, so that took her out of the equation. With a careful process of elimination, all fingers pointed to Azarah.

All of their problems began when she came into the picture. Then, what really took the cake for Dee Dee was how Azarah dealt with the police. No black girl she knew dealt with the police as if she was above them; unless she was one herself. Then she remembered two specific incidents that stuck out to her. One, was the day the detectives entered the store looking for 4Hunnid. She was real belligerent with the detectives. Then when one of them ran her name, he came back and almost had to drag the other detective out of the store, after telling Azarah she was good. The second incident happened two months ago while Azarah was taking her to the mall. They got pulled over for speeding. She was once again belligerent, but this time it was towards the not-so-nice county cops. Dee Dee was certain she would be driving Azarah's car to the mall, while she was being booked on disorderly conduct charges, but surprisingly the officer came back with her license, apologized for the inconvenience, and scurried off.

Then, her actions of late was uncomfortably questionable. Ever since the indictment was handed down, she had been acting weird. She moved her stuff from her room inside The Dungeon. She was always pulling disappearing acts, whereas no one can find her, and her phone is off. She no longer stayed in her house. Dee Dee tried following her one night after a girl's night out, but Azarah expertly lost her.

Dee Dee was convinced that Azarah was the police or was working for the police. And there was only one person who was skeptical about Azarah as she was.

"What's up Dee Dee?"

She jumped. "Boy, you scared me. Don't be walking up behind me like that without announcing yourself."

"My bad," Train said. "What'chu doing?"

"Listening to the songstress."

"Oh yeah."

"Yeah," Dee Dee said, stepping out of the doorway of the studio. "Let me ask you something Train?"

"What's up?" he asked, following her down the hallway.

"What'chu think about Azarah?"

Her question caught him off guard, and he was happy he was behind her so she couldn't see his reaction.

"What'chu mean, what I think?" he asked, thinking he was being tested.

She turned around to face him. "What I said, nigga. What do you think about the bitch?"

"Well you know, me and her never saw eye to eye. I never liked her. She seemed to come out of nowhere. I don't trust her."

"Me neither and two people feelings can't be wrong. Something is up with this bitch, and if I find out she got anything to do with them being locked up... I'll kill her."

A cold chill actually went down his spine as he looked Dee Dee in her eyes. He had never seen her so cold. She was always smiling and lively, but now she was cold blooded.

"I doubt that she got anything to do with them being in jail, Dee Dee."

"For her sake, I hope she didn't."

"You heard from any of them?" Train asked.

"Only through the lawyers. That shit is driving me crazy. They won't even use the phone."

"I got a homegirl over there that'll sneak them some cellphones in there."

She looked at him like he had four heads on his shoulders. "What makes ya silly-ass think they'll use cell phones in jail, if they didn't use them out here. Think Train."

"You right."

"We gotta do what we can from our end. We can find out who some of these informants is."

"Right. We can do that. I'm with that. Kill all rats!" Train yelled.

Back in the studio…

"It's good that you in pain Azarah. This shit is coming out amazing. You doing it right by turning this negative into a positive."

"But I miss him so much," she cried.

Sos'a got up to console her. "He gon' be aiight shorty. 4Hunnid is a strong dude."

"I know. I know."

"Jerrod is going to be proud of this album. I know he is," Taedo said. "Watch when he hears it."

"How we gon' get it to him?" she asked.

"We got ways," Sos'a said. "You can call it a day if you want to, Azarah. The album is done on your part. Me and Taedo gotta do our thing and then we'll be ready for distribution."

"Thanks guys. Love y'all."

"We love you too."

She walked upstairs quickly. She didn't like being in The Dungeon anymore, since everyone was locked up. The feeling wasn't the same anymore. She didn't feel right not smelling the pungent odor of marijuana that seemed to suffocate The Dungeon whenever everyone was working. It wasn't the same not seeing Jerrod walking around with his signature evil look and he could be having the best day of his life. She couldn't joke with Madd Lou about his height or playfully quiz Wild Bill on his gun knowledge. Magik wasn't around to bounce ideas off of. The Dungeon just wasn't The Dungeon to her no more. It felt more like a coffin.

She found Dee Dee and Tiffeny, the clerk, behind the counter.

"Dee Dee, you wanna get some lunch?"

"No," she said, nonchalantly.

Azarah caught the coldness in her 'no'. "What's wrong Dee?"

"Nothing."

She wasn't in the mood to deal with anyone else's emotions, with her own all over the place, so she left out to lunch by herself. She ended up on Boston Street in the Canton section of the city at the restaurant Sip & Bite.

As she took a seat, a wave of emotions swept over her body, causing her to burst into tears. She hadn't the slightest idea what was up with her emotions, but they was becoming harder to control. She cleaned herself up with the help of her Hermés compact mirror.

"Hi, my name is Paulette. Welcome to Sip & Bite of Canton. Can I interest you in an appetizer?"

"No thank-you Paulette. I'm ready to order."

"What would you like?"

"I would like the crab cake and shrimp."

"And how would you like your crab cake ma'am?"

"Broiled please."

"Anything else?"

"Yes, a Caesar salad please, and a freshly squoozed lemonade. That's it."

"Okay."

She was picking over her food when she saw Train's Benz drive by the restaurant.

"I told this boy to stay out of my business," she said, shaking her head, smiling. "He must've thought I was playing."

She slowly ate her food and then ordered a glass of wine to relax.

Her cell phone rung, just as she took the last sip of wine.

"Yes, mother... Out to lunch at Sip & Bite. Why?... Listen to what? ...What?!... I won't do it... What? Who?!... I don't know that name. I need more... Oh shit!... I won't do it," she said, and hung up.

She stood up and stumbled into the bathroom. She made it as far as the sink before she threw up her lunch. Her waitress came in and saw her bent over the sink. She rushed to her side and pulled her hair back so she wouldn't make more of a mess. She threw up some more. The waitress kept saying how sorry she was, and rubbing her back, thinking it was their food that made her sick.

The waitress escorted Azarah from the bathroom, ten minutes later, still apologizing.

"I'm okay. It wasn't the food."

"The meal is on us."

"I told you—"

"I won't hear no more of this. The meal is free."

Azarah was feeling woozy on the ride home. There was no way she would make it out 4Hunnid's house, where she had moved at once he got arrested, in her condition. Instead, she drove to her old house, where she still paid the bills.

She pulled up and staggered inside the house. She removed her clothes, and fell in her bed with her head spinning, and her stomach upset. It wasn't long before she was counting sheep.

When she opened her eyes, she was staring out over a sea of people that was staring at her. Directly in front of her was the angry faces of Magik, Madd Lou, Wild Bill, Jerrod, L-Trigga, DY, Nyse, Amil, Trina, and the love of her life; 4Hunnid, and all of their lawyers. Behind them was an abundance of fans, family, and press; watching her too. To her left was a box of thirteen people who looked at her through squinting eyes. They were all alert and woke; waiting attentively.

"We're waiting on you, Ms. Williams," a man said, from the right side of her.

She looked over at him and saw the man in the black robe, looking at her as well. "Well," he said.

"What was the question again?"

A white man stepped forward. "The question is; when did you take an interest in the Toe Tagging Posse Music Group?" he asked her. "Keep in mind, Quinetta Antionette Williams, that not only are you under oath, but you also took an oath to protect and serve."

"I won't do it! I won't do it! I won't do it!

She jumped up out of her sleep soaked in perspiration, breathing at a rapid pace. She looked at the clock. Seven hours had passed by. She got in the shower, washed away the day's problems, and contemplated her next step.

***

Magik & Trina's house…

"I wish you stop with the worrying Amil."

"Why shouldn't I be? You getting on my nerves with this laid-back attitude of yours Trina. You are charged with distribution."

"My man said we good, so we good."

"Speaking of him. Everyone is convinced that he had lost his mind over the jail. They say he doesn't study the case like everyone else. They say when they meet every week to discuss their game plan, he just remains silent. When they ask him what's wrong, he always says that what they doing is for nothing and that everyone is going home; treat it like a vacation."

"They should listen to him."

Amil looked at Trina like she was crazy. "Trina, they are asking for the death penalty for Wild Bill, Lou, Nyse, and 4Hunnid."

"Calm down Amil. Everyone is coming home."

"The shit you saying is ludicrous, Trina! All my fuckin' accounts are frozen! They are trying to say I was laundering money for Jerrod."

It was Trina's turn to look at Amil like she was crazy.

"Are we losing you, Amil?" Trina asked, removing her nickel plated, pearl handle .380 from her dip and placed it on the table. "We don't need no discord in the family."

"You really gonna pull a gun on me, Trina?"

"I would never. It was hurting my stomach," she said, picking the gun back up. She pointed the pretty handgun at Amil's head. "This is pulling a gun on you, Amil."

Tears ran down Amil's pretty face. "I can't believe you, Trina. We've been friends since the second grade."

"I'm apart of something that's bigger than our friendship Amil; a family."

"I'm apart of that same family."

Trina sat the gun back down. "I 'on't know Amil. You acting like you scared right now."

"Acting? I am scared. But what does that have to do with anything?"

"It has everything to do with everything. Fear makes people do stupid shit."

"Are you insinuating that I'll tell on Jerrod?"

"I'm not insinuatin' shit. Like I said, fear makes people do stupid shit."

"I'm no street girl, but I'm no rat either," she cried.

Trina walked over to Amil and hugged her. "Trust me boo, no one is going to jail. The boys are on vacation. We will be back together. We just have to be here for one another. It's mandatory. That means no more private meetings with your lawyer and the prosecutor. Okay? Can you honor that Amil?

"Yes. I can."

* * *

Clearance Mitchell Jr. Courthouse…

Prosecutor Criag Scott sat at the large oak table in front of stacks of papers, with detectives Talia Coppola, Jerkman 'Jerk' Travoski, Ernie 'Erk' Jarvos, and Swain Lin.

"Okay, so we got an air tight case against Davenport on this murder of Cardwell (Speedy) —"

"Not Cardwell. It's Lawrence Weathers (Traum)," Erk corrected him.

"So what happened with the drug addict who said he brought drugs for Davenport from the house—"

"He's not willing to testify," Coppola said.

"So, we have him on Weathers' murder?"

"Yup. I'm testifying and the sister, Lisa Weathers, is testifying as well. We got that one in the bag."

"What's our chances on flipping one of the co-defendants?" Lin asked.

"We tried the accountant, DeCario, but she wasn't budging. We pulled out every trick in the book. She cried, but she stood tall," Scott said. "But we don't need no one to flip. Our undercover and our confidential informant in their immediate circle is all we need," Scott smiled, knowing this case would score him major points with the big wigs and make him a shoe-in for the head prosecutor. "This case is in the bag."

***

(The Next Day)
The Dungeon...
"Damn girl, you look like hell," Flee said, as Azarah walked pass him. "Yo singing today?"

"No," she said. "You seen Dee Dee?"

"No. She didn't even open up the store today; Tiffeny did."

"Don't she normally open up the store?"

"Normally?" Tommy Gunz said, coming out of the kitchen with a steaming cup of coffee. "She's the only one who opens the store. She don't open it, it don't open. I asked Tiffeny how she got the keys, and she said Dee Dee left the key in her mailbox with a note telling her to open the store, because she was going out of town."

"And that didn't sound weird to you?" Azarah asked.

"It's a lot of weird shit that's been going on around here since you got here."

Her head snapped back at neck breaking speed. "And you saying that, to say what nigga?"

"Don't get feisty with me. I'm just stating the obvious. These niggas been sellin' drugs, shootin' and killin' niggas before Toe Taggin' Posse was even thought about, and never had a problem before little Ms. Azarah came along."

"Come out and say what'chu tryna say, Tommy?"

"The truth don't need no explanation, Azarah."

"Suck my pussy, pussy," she shouted in anger, and left Flee and Tommy Gunz standing there.

"That girl ain't right, Flee."

"If that's true, and Jerrod is ya man, why is she able to not be right?"

"What'chu sayin' Flee?"

"I ain't sayin' nothin' Gunz. I'm just the DJ," Flee said, and went inside the studio.

***

Baltimore City Detention Center…

4Hunnid gave his hall pass to the CO at the visiting door and then went into the bullpen to wait for his name to be called for a visit. He noticed a few guys off in the corner huddled up freestyling. He walked over close to them to listen. The other guys in the bullpen started paying attention as well. They knew who 4Hunnid was. He hadn't spit one rhyme since he got locked up. It was obvious he missed it.

He bobbed his head to the rhymes the guy was spitting. The guy saw 4Hunnid and included him and Toe Taggin' Posse in his freestyle, out of respect. In the freestyling world that was an invite into the cipher. 4Hunnid was in a good mood, so he joined in.

Bitch I'm me, Baltimore's gangsta
4Hunnid Ru, born in to danger
Trouble is my friend, I ain't really into strangers
Clip full of wings, turn ya boys in to angels
Shoot'chu in yo' halo, shoot you like Halo
Bodymore's A-hole,
Free my nigga Kayo All about my bread like
bagels, they know I'm raw like qualos,
my aim right like HO's Ah nigga so strong it's like I
twist tornados
Spit like nines, four-fifths and three eight o's
Niggas want problems, well I am problematic

*It's back to pickin' cotton cause you niggas cotton
candy*
I'mma Tree Top Piru, deep water Shammu
Shoot you from ya Head to ya Shoulders; shampoo
Fuck in ah bamboo, fuck in bedroom
Pass that bitch down like ah heirloom
Yeah, 4Hunnid, Toe Taggin' Posse, woop woop

"Your visit is here 4Hunnid," the CO said.

4Hunnid dapped the guys up in the cipher and walked in the visiting room. He saw the love of his life on the other side of the glass and smiled.

"Hey sexy."

"Hey handsome," she said.

One look at her and he knew she had a reason for coming.

"How are you?"

"Do you trust me, bae?" she asked.

"I guess you're not doing too good. I'm fine. We are fine."

"That's not answering my question. Do you trust me?" she asked, with tears welling up in he eyes.

"I have no choice but to trust you," he said.

"King, I have something to tell you."

4Hunnid looked her in the eyes. He could count on both hands the amount of people he trusted in his life. It was how he lasted so long in the game.

"Does this have anything to do with the case?" 4Hunnid asked.

She nodded her head, as the tears fell down her face.

"You know what I told you, right?" She nodded again.

"I meant that. No talking about the case at all. Under no circumstances."

"But this could h—"

"No circumstances Azarah. Let me ask you this though: are you loyal to me?"

"Four hunnid percent."

"Then what's understood don't need to be explained," he said, got up and left out of the visiting room.

At the same time Wild Bill was coming from out of the visit from the lawyer side.

"4Hunnid!"

"Bill, what's up my nigga?"

"Man, I just came from seeing my lawyer."

4Hunnid looked around for a private place to talk.

There wasn't any.

"Here, take y'all's passes. If y'all wanna talk in private, go in the hallway. If someone come, walk up the steps like y'all just left out of here."

"Thanks Ms. Green."

"No problem."

They went out in the hallway.

"What's good?"

"We start trial next week."

"What'cha lawyer saying? How shit looking?" 4Hunnid asked.

(Sighed) "My lawyer ain't sounding or looking confident."

"Same as my aunt. I can tell that it's all bad. What's up with Magik over there?"

"Man, me and him was ready to fight the other night. That nigga has completely lost his mind. He's too happy, bruh. Like this shit is a joke. I keep telling that nigga this ain't ah game. Yo, he just on some bullshit. I think he going for the crazy role. Too unstable to stand trial or some shit like that."

"Huh? You think so? Really?"

"I know it's hard to believe, but it's only because you not over there with him. I'm telling you bruh, he's gone; mentally."

"He aiight."

"If you say so." Wild Bill sighed. "Who came down to see you?"

"Azarah. She on her female, emotional shit."

"How you holding up bruh? These folks really tryna kill us," Wild Bill said.

"I'm good bruh. To tell you the truth Bill, I don't even think about that shit. It doesn't bother me none. I lived a helluva life, my nigga. Straight rockstar, gangsta lifestyle," he laughed. "How you feelin'?"

"I wouldn't feel so bad about it if I didn't have this happy-go-lucky-ass nigga Magik in the cell with me." 4Hunnid laughed. "That shit ain't funny bruh. You don't know what I be going through over there with that nigga."

"Regardless of how this shit ends Bill, we did it as men," 4Hunnid said. "Toe Taggin' Posse." He twisted his fingers up.

Wild Bill did the same. "TTP," he said.

CHAPTER 27
Trial Time People

Their trial was treated like one of their concerts; with a ton of media coverage. Channels 2 (ABC), 13 (WJZ), 11 (WBAL), and 45 (FOX), was all there to cover the trial of the year. Because the judge wanted to deter other kingpins, drug dealers, gangsters, and rap crews from criminal acts, he made the call to allow cameras inside the courtroom, so that the trial was televised.

The governor gave several press conferences on the Toe Taggin' Posse Music Group's trial. In one press conference, he brung Coppola, Travoski, and Jarvos up to the podium to personally thank them for all of their hard work, on taking the violent, murderous rap group off the streets. The IITSU detectives ate the recognition up and never got tired of hearing: "Congratulations", "Good job", and "IITSU is the best".

The prison-van pulled up on the side of the courthouse. The reporters got their cameras ready. Their fans covered the whole block, but was held back by the police and concrete barriers.

"Y'all's fifteen minutes of fame begins when you hop off this van," Big Van, the transportation CO, said.

"You got us fucked up Big Van," 4Hunnid said. "You see all these ma'fuckas out here? Our fame started way before this court shit. We were born with fame," he chuckled, nervously. He wouldn't admit it; ever, but he was nervous as hell. Him and his co-defendants were. They all felt like cows being led to the slaughter house.

Their style of dress was out of sync of sorts. L-Trigga, Nyse, DY, Jerrod, and Wild Bill were impeccably dressed in taylor-made suits. Madd Lou and 4Hunnid settled for Nike boots, black Robbin jeans, and black Lacosté shirts; explaining that they were at war and needed to be dressed as so. Magik on the other hand, was another story. He dressed like he was going to the club. Jordan #9s, red True Religion shirt, and a pair of True Religion jeans. The rest of them didn't care, so long as he wasn't acting crazy. For some strange reason, after they picked the jury last week his demeanor had gotten serious. They just chalked it up as reality settling-in in him.

"Damn, I know the store has sold out. Look at all the family with our clothes on"

"Oh, I forgot to tell y'all; the store is bone dry. The family bought every item we had in the store. Amil said the governor saying that our accounts were frozen, actually helped the store. Our fans/family thought we was broke, and started a Instagram page in our name and came out in droves to support us. They had a show in the parking lot of Toe Taggin' Attire. Young Moose, Lor Scoota, Gutta, Lano, Hunnid Gran, E-Watts all performed," Jerrod said.

"That was some real-nigga-shit," 4Hunnid said.

"Anybody heard from Dee Dee?"

"Naw Lou. I haven't."

"That's crazy. That ain't Dee Dee."

The CO's got out of the van with their shotguns. Some extra police came out of the side of the courthouse and surrounded the van.

"Y'all ready," Big Van asked, opening the door.

Jerrod was led out first, shackled, chained, and handcuffed, just like the rest of them. Magik was the next to be led off. The crowd screamed his name, clapped, and whistled. Nyse got out and yelled, "Was'sup wit'ch'all dumbasses?" The crowd screamed back, "Was'sup wit'cha dumbass, Nyse?" He threw his head up in recognition of his loyal fans. Wild Bill followed him. Madd Lou got out next.

"Madd Lou! We love you!" a group of women yelled from behind the barriers. He looked and smiled at the seven women who had on 'Free The 5 Feet Assassin' shirts on. L-Trigga and Dummy Yummy was next. The crowd began chanting, "Park Heights Bitch!" out of love for the two Park Heights gangsters.

A group off to the right was throwing 'L's in the air out of their Love, Loyalty & Lanes for their big homie L-Trigga. The crowd got deafly loud as 4Hunnid scooted up to be helped off the van. He threw his head back to get his dreads out of his face. He wanted to see the love the streets had for him and his brothers. When he stepped off the van, they got even louder. They chanted everything under the sun for their beloved, energetic rapper.

The CO's purposely held them up on the sidewalk as the reporters, fans, and family took pictures and recorded videos.

***

Conference Room #4...

Kia Perry (Jerrod's lawyer), Connie Yarborough (4Hunnid's lawyer), Lawerence Rosenburg (Madd Lou's lawyer), Christie Needleman (Wild Bill's lawyer), Ivan Bates (DY's lawyer), John Hassett (Nyse's lawyer), Margret Meed (Amil's lawyer), Howard Cardeen (Trina's lawyer), Ron Caroline (L-Trigga's lawyer), and Kenneth Ravenel (Magik's lawyer), all sat around the table discussing strategy over hot cups of coffee.

"I have no problem with you running point, Connie, but what direction are you pushing the wind?" Meed asked.

"Since it's all circumstantial, I'm aiming for discrediting the witnesses. We'll see how well or bad things are going before we regroup."

"I'm telling you all now, don't be surprised when I don't cross examine no one."

"What's that suppose to mean, Ravenel?" Connie Y asked.

"Nothing. I've been instructed to only cross examine my client and his girlfriend."

"And she told me that I am not to cross examine her and that you, Ravenel, would be the only one questioning her," Cardeen said.

"Then it's settled."

"What type of hooky-pook shit is this?" Hassett asked.

"That doesn't sound right."

"I agree with Hassett," Meed said. "This sounds like some underhanded stuff."

"Why don't you just tell us your angle Ravenel?" Perry said, tapping her manicured finger tips on the table.

"Trust me, I thought my client was crazy too. This is what he wants, and this is what he paid me to do. So, I must do it."

"This is bullshit! I told Harvey to get a severance."

"Okay, okay. No need to fall apart here," Connie Y said. "I have one question Ravenel."

"Okay."

"Is what you're doing going to hurt anyone else's case?"

"Not even a little bit."

"Then let's proceed," she said. "We have a tough one ahead of us guys. Let's stay focused."

There was a knock at the door. Ivan Bates answered it. It was the bailiff.

"Excuse my interruption, but your clients are here."

"Thanks Norman," Connie Y said. "Let's go gang."

Everyone stood up.

"You better not say 'gang' too loud around here. Lord knows I don't need the trouble," Kia Perry said, causing everyone to burst into laughter.

The first day of trial was mostly Judge Rodger Gibson giving the jury (four black women, two white women, five white men, one white woman, and the two extras were black men) instructions and what to expect.

The second day was opening statements for the state. The states attorney, Criag Scott, painted a mental picture of a murderous rap crew, who had not even an ounce of respect for human life. He promised to prove how the Toe Taggin' Posse Music Group was able to finance the biggest rap label in the state of Maryland. He said he would show how they were able to acquire two Bentleys, seven Benz's, four penthouses, seven large homes, numerous businesses; including Toe Taggin' Attire. He also claimed he would prove how two different gangs put their differences aside, and formed a more profitable gang, all in the name of money.

He talked for an hour. The rest of the day was half of the defense attorney's opening statements. On the third day, the other five defense attorneys gave their opening statements. The fourth day is when the war actually started. The state called their first witness.

***

On day four the co-defendants walked in the courtroom. As soon as the COs began taking their chains off, 4Hunnid looked around the courtroom. He didn't see Azarah. He looked down the bench at Trina. She knew what he wanted. She just shrugged her shoulders. She didn't know where Azarah was. They had rode together the first three days, but this morning she didn't see her, nor was she answering her phone.

"All rise," the bailiff said. "Judge Rodger Gibson presiding over case number two seven four six six eight four."

Judge Gibson sat down. "You may be seated. State, call your first witness."

"Yes, Your Honor. The state would like to call Wong Tong."

The courtroom doors opened and in walked a 4'11", stocky, Asian man. Jerrod just shook his head.

"State your name for the courts."

"My name is Wong Tong," he said, in broken English.

"And where are you from Wong Tong?"

"Myanmar, Southeast Asia."

"Why were you in Baltimore, Mr. Tong?"

"I was on run from country."

"Your country?" Scott asked.

"Yes."

"And when did you reach Baltimore?"

"Seven months long."

"You've been here for seven months?" He shook his head. "And what did you do to survive here in Baltimore?"

"I sold heroin to Freddy," Wong Tong said, looking at Jerrod.

"And who is Freddy?" Scott asked. He pointed to Jerrod. "Let the record reflect, the witness has pointed out Jerrod Frampton."

Wong Tong testified for an hour straight. He testified that he was a direct descendant of Myanmar's Prince of Death; Khun Sa, and that was how he was able to amass such large quantities of heroin to sell to Freddy/Jerrod.

After Wong Tong stepped down, the state called their next witness; a drug expert, then some officers that knew Jerrod from back in the day. The day was pretty much over after they took the stand.

Jerrod wasn't worried until they began talking about old murders he committed. They didn't shake him, but it did bother him.

***

Day fifteen of the trial and they were getting worried. The state was putting on a brilliant show. They could honestly have closing arguments, now, and get unanimous guilty verdicts all the way across the board. The defense needed some points up on the board... bad.

It wasn't helping that no one had heard a peep from Dee Dee, and Azarah was now missing too. 4Hunnid was so concerned that he broke his own rule and called Tommy Gunz from the jail phone.

"Hello."

"TG, this me, 4Hunnid."

Tommy Gunz was shocked. "What's up my nigga?"

"I know it's surprising, but this important."

"What's up?"

"I need to find my girl. You seen her?"

"Nope. Trina just asked me the same shit when I saw her earlier."

"Damn, where the fuck is this girl," he said, in frustration.

"If I see her, I'll tell her to call Connie Y."

"Good lookin' out my nigga."

"Other than the obvious, how you?"

"I'm good. You know me Gunz. I'm built Ford tough."

(Chuckled) "I know. Y'all gon' be aiight. We'll be back together making music soon."

"You already [sic]," 4Hunnid said, and heard someone holler his name in the background.

"Yo, Train holla'd at'chu."

"Tell Train Smoke I love him, and hold the fort down."

"I heard you my nigga. You on speaker. I miss y'all niggas man. I can't wait until y'all beat this shit."

"Me either. Yo, I'm 'bout to rest up for court tomorrow. I love y'all niggas man."

"We love you too, 4Hunnid," they both said.

"Too Taggin'," 4Hunnid said, and hung up.

"So what happened bruh?" Madd Lou asked, when he walked up to him.

"Gunz or Train ain't seen her. I 'on't know what the fuck going on bruh. First Dee Dee, now Azarah."

"Don't let that shit bother you 4Hunnid. We still got a big ass road block ahead of us."

"I know Lou, but I can't help but worry. Looney Redz still out there with all his friends dead. That nigga probably got'em."

"If you that worried, one call, message, or note to the homies, and his ass is outta here."

"I just might do that Madd Lou. I'm going to get in the shower."

***

Day 16 of trial…

"Call your witness state."

"Yes, Your Honor," Prosecutor Scott said. "State would like to call Sergeant Major Lisa Weathers."

She walked in the courtroom confidently. Even in her army issued BDUs she commanded attention with her beauty."

4Hunnid looked at her, almost regretting settling for the fellatio.

"Good morning, Sergeant Major."

"Good morning, Mr. Scott, and Ms. Weathers is fine."

"Fine, Ms. Weathers it is," he said. "You're here today because—"

"I object Your Honor; leading," Connie Y said.

"Why are you here today, Ms. Weathers?"

"Because I witnessed my oldest brother's murder."

"Can you tell the jury what you saw?"

"Yes. I was walking to my brother's car with my little brother. By the time we got to the car, my oldest brother, Lawrence Weathers, was coming out of the house. I looked back at my brother and saw a look of horror on his face. I followed his line of sight and by that time he, my brother, had took off running. A person in all black ran past me with a gun and started shooting at my brother. A car sped past us in pursuit of the gunman and my brother. I didn't see much else, but I heard the shots."

"Did you get a good look at the shooter, Ms. Weathers?"

"No. Whoever it was, had a mask on."

"Lets back up a minute. Were you aware of any problems, if any, that Lawrence may have been having?"

"Before I came back from Iraq, I was aware of a sibling beef between my brothers. My father had wrote me and told me about it."

"So your brothers were at odds?"

"I object. Ms. Weathers just answered that," Connie Y said.

"Get to the point Mr. Scott," Judge Gibson said, running his hand threw his all white hair.

"Was that the only problem Lawrence had, Ms. Weathers?"

"No. The day I got back in the city, my father called Loo-Leonard, my younger brother and his girl, over for dinner. When we sat down and Lawrence came up from the basement, Leonard jumped up and threatened to leave. My father made them both sit down and eat. After we ate, my father made them both stay seated and iron out their differences."

"Did they iron out their differences?"

"Yes."

"And how do you know, Ms. Weathers?"

"Because, I was back and forth eavesdropping on their conversation."

"Can you remember what you heard?"

"I object, Your Honor. Ms. Weathers said she was back and forth eavesdropping on their conversation. Which means she didn't hear the entire conversation."

"Overruled," the judge said.

"You may answer my question, Ms. Weathers," Prosecutor Scott said.

"I heard my brother, Leonard, fussing at Lawrence about being a snitch. I heard Lawrence defending his name. He began telling Leonard about a police being inside of Toe Tagging Posse Music Group. My father had called me to do something, so I walked off. When I came back, I could tell the tension had died down. My brother Lawrence, who also went by Traum, was confiding in my brother Leonard, who also goes by Looney, about a kidnapping that him and a friend of his, Dun Deal, committed. The guy they kidnapped got away and his homeboy Dun Deal was killed."

"Do you know the name of the person your brother supposedly kidnapped?"

"No. I didn't hear a name."

"Do you know any of the ten defendants, sitting her today?"

She looked over all of them. "I don't know any of them personally."

"But you've seen them before?"

"Objection," Connie Y said.

"Sustained."

"Okay. Have you seen any of them before?"

"Yes. I've seen one of them before."

"Which one Ms. Weathers?"

"Him," she pointed.

"Let the record reflect that Ms. Weathers has pointed out King Davenport aka 4Hundred," the prosecutor said.

"Where and when did you see him?"

"Outside of my brother's house, two days before he was killed."

"What was he doing?" he asked, and she proceeded to give him the same story she gave the detectives at Looney's house. "So he told you his name was KT and he asked you for directions?"

"Yes."

"That's it?"

"Yes," she said, with a straight face.

"And you've never—"

"Objection Your Honor."

"Sustained."

"Have you ever saw Mr. Davenport before that day?"

"No."

"What about afterwards, Ms. Weathers?"

"No," she said, with a straight face.

"Are you positive that Mr. Davenport is the one who presented himself to you as KT, on your brother's block two days before Lawrence's murder?"

"I'm one hundred percent sure."

"Nothing further, Your Honor."

"Defense," Judge Gibson said.

Connie Y stood up and smoothed her Stella McCartney business, suit skirt down. "Ms. Weathers, how long have you been in the Army?"

"Six years."

"And what is it that the Army taught you?"

"Objection, Your Honor," the prosecutor said.

"As to what Mr. Scott?"

"Irrelevancy, You Honor."

"Ms. Yarborough, are you going somewhere in your questioning?"

"Yes, if Mr. Scott would allow me to."

"Don't get cute Ms. Yarborough. I told you and the others, my courtroom will not become a circus," Judge Gibson warned. "Now, your objection Mr. Scott is overruled. You may proceed."

The TV news cameras caught Connie Y's scowl.

"What had the Army taught you, Ms. Weathers?"

"A lot of things. Discipline. Respect. Honor. Loyalty."

"What about honesty, Ms. Weathers?" Connie Y asked, half expecting Lisa to come clean.

Instead of being honest, she said, "They didn't have to teach me that, because it was already in me."

"Is that right?"

"Yes."

146

Connie Y went to the defense table and picked up some papers. "When you were explaining what happened on the day of your brother's murder, you described the person that ran pass you shooting, as a person. Is that right?"

"Yes. Like I said, I didn't see the person. So it could've been a man or woman."

"Okay, let's jump off track a bit here. Prosecutor Scott asked you, did you know any of the accused. I'm going to ask you again, but I'm going to be more specific."

"Objection. She already said she didn't know any of them," Scott argued.

"Overruled."

"Sergeant Major Lisa Weathers, do you personally, or any other kind of way, know any of the accused?"

"No, I don't," she lied, with a straight face.

"Do you wear glasses, Ms. Weathers?"

"No, I have twenty-twenty vision."

"Keep in mind that you are under oath, Ms. Weathers."

"I know that."

"Look at my client, King Davenport. Are you telling me and the court that you don't know my client?"

She hesitated for a minute, but she had already gone too far, so she just kept up with her lies. "No, I don't know him, other than giving him directions that day."

"So you never went out on a dinner date with my client?" she asked, shocking everyone in the courtroom.

Prosecutor Scott couldn't believe what he heard.

Connie Y passed her a piece of paper. "Can you tell the court what that is?"

She looked it over. "It's a receipt for Kobe Japanese Steakhouse. So, I always go there when I come home," she said, shrugging it off.

"Read the receipt Ms. Weathers."

"Kobe fried rice. Seafood combination. Filet mignon, Lobster. And the house wine."

"Did you go alone?"

"I don't remember."

"Tell the court the date on the receipt."

"It's two days before my brother's murder," she said.

"Yes. The same day you claim my client asked you for directions, right."

"Correct."

"How is it that you can remember my client asking for directions; on this same day, and remember what happened two days later, but don't remember who you went to dinner with?"

"I don't know."

"Perhaps the Army taught you how to lie."

"Objection."

"Sustained. Move on Ms. Yarborough."

"Yes, Your Honor. I'm almost done," she said, going back to the defense table. She grabbed a disc. "Your Honor, I'd like to play Exhibit 17 to maybe jog the memory of Ms. Weathers."

"May we approach Your Honor?" Prosecutor Scott asked.

"Yes," he said.

"Your Honor, I've never seen this disc before."

"I don't see why not, I have," the judge said, "and it shows that your client is a liar and I fully intend to lock her up for perjury, when she's done on the witness stand. Not only does she know Mr. Davenport, but she also, excuse my language Ms. Yarborough, performed fellatio on him."

"No offense taken."

"This is not an open and shut case. You are going up against the toughest, roughest, most intelligent, and the most skillful attorneys in Baltimore City."

Connie Y gave the disc to the bailiff, who put it in the computer, so that it would show up on the big screen. He pressed play. It was a tape of one of the surveillance cameras inside of the steakhouse. Everyone watched as Lisa and 4Hunnid entered the establishment, laughing. After a while, their food was served. Connie Y paused it.

"Ms. Weathers, can you tell me and the courts, what's that on the table?"

"Kobe fried rice, the seafood combination, filet mignon, and a lobster."

"Okay," Connie Y said, and pressed play.

Once they left out of the steakhouse the disc switched over to a homemade video that 4Hunnid recorded on his digital camera. From the audio, they heard 4Hunnid's verse off of him and Madd Lou's song, *Four My Hood*. The next thing they saw sent shockwaves throughout the courtroom. Prosecutor Scott objected to the video, claiming they all got the point, but his plea was overruled and they all watched the video in it's entirety.

Lisa couldn't watch it. She placed her head in her hand, embarrassingly.

"Do you remember my client now, Ms. Weathers?"

"Yes, I do."

"Can you speak up? We can't hear you."

"Yes. I know him."

"So why lie?"

"I don't know."

"Not only did you know Mr. Davenport, but you performed a sexual act on him," Connie said. "Did he call you after that night?"

"No."

"How did that make you feel?"

"Like I blew it. I went too far, too soon."

"Was you mad?"

"At him; a little bit. At myself a lot."

"The person that ran pass you, shooting at your brother, could that have been—"

"Objection, Your Honor. She's not an expert in observation."

"Sustained."

"The person that ran pass you, you described as husky. Is that correct?"

"Yes."

She turned around to the defense table. "Mr. Davenport, can you please stand up?" 4Hunnid stood up. "Is this husky to you, Ms. Weathers?"

"No."

"Nothing further Your Honor."

Kia Perry stood up. "So you lied about knowing Mr. Davenport?"

"Yes."

"Under oath?" Kia Perry asked, making sure Lisa Weathers secured a spot in a jail cell for perjury.

"Yes."

"Nothing further Your Honor," she said, and sat back down.

"State?"

(Sighed) "Nothing further Your Honor," Prosecutor Scott said, not wanting to make matters worse.

"You may step down... but do not leave," the judge warned. "Call your next witness."

"The state would like to call Detective Ernie Jarvos."

Detective Ernie "Erk" Jarvos walked through the doors of the courtroom with a too tight shirt on, some baggy jeans, and some sandals. It took everything in the defendants not to burst out laughing at him. A few of the jurors wasn't as strong as them, and laughed out loud.

"Order in the court!" the judge said, and banged the gavel. "Mr. Jarvos, is your shirt tight enough?"

"Yes, sir," he said, nervously.

After he got sworn in, Prosecutor Scott began pacing in front of him.

"How long have you been a police officer, Detective Jarvos?"

"Ten years."

"Can you explain the unit you work for now?"

"I work in the IITS Unit, which stands for Industry In The Streets, and we're basically a unit similar to the Hip Hop Police. We monitor individuals that's in the industry, and if we believe or get intel that a person or group's art is imitating life, we start investigating. If it turns up to be nothing, we stop, and it's on to the next one."

"And can you tell us how did you come to meet the Toe Tagging Posse Music Group?"

"Of course," he said, smiling, remembering the day clearly. "My partners Talia Coppola, Jerkman Travoski, and myself were assigned to a group named Slaughtermore."

"It was in June of twenty twelve at 92Q's Summer Jam concert, at Druid Hill Park. My partners and I was close to the stage when the crowd started getting unruly, and screaming, and threatening to break the barriers. Our backs were towards the stage, so we had no idea that it was anyone up there, then the music dropped."

"We turned around and saw; 4Hundred, Madd Lou, Magik, and Wild Bill. It was our first glimpse at them. We had heard of their emergence on the radio and through intel. We heard they were slated to dethrone Slaughtermore, and it was clear, because the crowd loved them."

"That day, I started my investigation out of curiousness. I wanted to know where they came from. In my initial investigation, I found that they were signed to a label called Toe Taggin' Posse, that was owned by Jerrod Frampton. Jerrod Frampton, I have heard of from older officers. He was a ruthless drug dealer back in the nineties—"

"Objection, Your Honor. Speculation."

"Sustained."

"Stick to the facts, Detective Jarvos."

"Yes. Once I found out who was behind the Toe Tagging Posse, I dug deeper. Knowing Frampton was a self proclaimed member of the Tree Top Pirus, I began looking at the artists on the label. I found out from our gang log book, that they too were members of Tree Top Piru. It wasn't that farfetched with a label named Toe Tagging Posse. TTP is TTP however you use it."

"When you began looking into the artists on Toe Tagging Posse Music Group, what did you find?"

"Not surprisingly, nothing."

"Nothing?"

"Not one thing. They were rappers, who rapped for money. They did shows, they got paid."

"You sound like there's a 'but' somewhere."

"But, I wasn't buying the rapper act," Erk said. "I went to talk to someone in the gang task force to get some intel on the inner workings of TTP. At that point I only heard of TTP. I heard about the '06 case, all the alleged acts of violence against police officers, and the corruption. The gang task force officer that I spoke to, warned me about the cunningness of this particular gang. He described them as ruthless, heartless, intelligent, entrepreneurs. His words proved to be true…"

Prosecutor Scott questioned Erk extensively about his dealings with Toe Taggin' Posse artists. Scott believed he accomplished his mission in painting the picture of some ruthless, gang banging rappers. He pounded the words *Art Imitates Life* into the juror's head. After Erk was excused from the stand, Prosecutor Scott played various tracks from the Toe Taggin' Posse artist, Nyse, and DY.

The prosecutor then put four snitches on the stand to testify against L-Trigga. They all claimed they purchased more than one hundred grams from him at various events that was hosted by his company Kode of Silence.

The next day the state put on their case against Nyse. They had numerous people testify on Nyse's insanity. They had ten people testify who knew Nyse. They all told some bizarre story of Nyse's acts of violence. Of the ten, one was Carey Street's neighborhood prostitute; Cola. Surprisingly, she didn't tell about the murder Nyse committed in front of her, but she told about all the guns he stashed in her house, the drugs, and everything she heard him discussing.

The state was putting on an excellent case. Their death penalty case was looking good and Prosecutor Scott was ecstatic. He just knew the number one prosecutor job was his and the best was yet to come.

Traitor Tellin' Pussy

The state's case was finally winding down. Prosecutor Scott was confident in his progress thus far, but he planned to seal his victory with his next trick.

The Toe Taggin' co-defendants and affiliates were beyond stressed. They remained calm and cool in the face of adversity, but back at the jail they smoked themselves silly; everyone except Magik that is. He was still himself. He didn't change one bit. He kept a smile on his face at the jail.

One month into trial and still none of them had heard from Dee Dee or Azarah. No one said it out loud, but they were all half-expecting Azarah to take the stand on them.

Dee Dee was another story. They had no idea where she was. It was totally out of character for her to pull a disappearing act. They knew 400% that in

KAYO | BREAKING NEWS 2

some way, shape, form, or fashion she was being detained against her will, or she would've at least called Tommy Gunz, Trina, Train, or Amil.

4Hunnid had sent a message to Amil and Trina through Connie Y to find Azarah and Dee Dee. They sent a message back, that their search was fruitless; both of their homes looked like they were empty. Trina called in some help from a few Tree Top homies and had them sitting on the houses. The Toe Taggin' Posse was beyond worried.

***

It was the thirty-third day of trial and the state was set to bring their case to a close and let the defense have a turn. The exhaustion was apparent on the faces of the accused. Even Magic was showing signs of fatigue.

They were led in the courtroom. Their shackles, cuffs, and chains were removed, then the reporters were led in, along with their family members and supporters. The court reporter and bailiff came in at exactly eight am.

"All rise," the bailiff said.

The judge came in, gave his normal instructions, and gave the floor to Prosecutor Scott.

"The state would like to call..."

The state's next witness came in and dropped the mouths of all ten accused affiliates and members of the Toe Taggin' Posse. This witness came out of left field. Now they understood why the state fought so hard to keep the witness list concealed. They looked at the witness with such disdain, if looks could kill...

The prosecutor approached the witness box in an effort to calm his witness down. He saw nothing but fear written on the witness' face.

"How are you today?"

"I'm nervous," he chuckled, wiping sweat beads from his forehead.

"What is your relationship to Toe Tagging Posse Music Group?"

"You mean what **was** my relationship to them?" he countered, nervously.

"Yes, was."

"I was the A&R of the company. I went out and found the talent for the company."

"And were you the one who brought Magik, 4Hunnid, Madd Lou, and Wild Bill to the Toe Tagging Posse Music Group?"

"No. They were the Genesis of Toe Taggin' Posse. They came with Jerrod. The record company was my idea. Jerrod was the money I needed, so I went to him with the idea, and he was with it."

"And how did you meet Jerrod?" Prosecutor Scott asked.

"I knew him through a cousin of mine who got killed. We actually met at the funeral. Him and my cousin use to get money together, sellin' dope. I knew he had some money, so I waited a few weeks before I came to him with my idea."

"What made you present it to him?"

"Like I said, he had money. Old money. Dope money."

"When you presented it to him, what did he say?"

"My cousin was my heart, and I'm assuming he knew that, and being as though my cousin was his heart, if I wanted to open a chicken coop, he would've probably been with it. But when I presented it to him, he was ecstatic. I had the knowledge and he had the money. He also had the artists to take the company where we wanted it to go."

"Who named the record label?"

"Jerrod. It shouldn't be a secret that Toe Taggin' Posse is a acronym for TTP. The whole Baltimore know what TTP stands for; Tree Top Piru. He always said, the music group's name is a way to pay homage to the hood."

"You say you were around since the inception of Toe Tagging Posse Music Group, did you ever see anything illegal?"

"All the time. Everyday."

"Can you elaborate please?"

"For instance, they nicknamed me Tommy Gunz, but him right there, he was the gunman. That boy had hella guns."

"Let the record reflect that the witness has pointed out Louis Ramsey aka Madd Lou."

"I don't believe I ever saw him with the same gun twice in the whole two and ah half years I've known him. And most of the guns were bigger than him," he said, really getting into emptying his brain in open court.

"What did you do when you saw the guns?"

"If I found them in his room at Toe Taggin' Attire, I would take them and turn them in to the police."

"And how many guns have you stolen from Mr. Ramsey?"

"Eleven."

"Did he ever get suspicious?"

"Of course, he did. See, Dee Dee hated guns in her store and she told us to keep them out of her establishment. The boys looked up to her as a big sister, so I used that as my cover. Every time Madd Lou would ask me, I'd tell'em Dee Dee was in his room. I knew he wouldn't question her."

"Did you see anything else?"

"I've witnessed big drug deals go down."

"By who?"

"Jerrod. I knew Jerrod supplied L-Trigga, Nyse, DY, as well as the Toe Taggin' Posse. I witnessed Jerrod hand L-Trigga and Nyse four kilos ah piece that was vacuum-sealed and wrapped in black paper. These are certified dope boys. Smart ones at that."

"What do you mean by that?"

"They weren't like any dope boys I ever met. They never used phones. They never spoke about their drug dealing outside of the conference room inside The Dungeon. They handled their business, made great music, and had fun."

Prosecutor Scott questioned him for another forty-five minutes and then let the defense at him.

Kia Perry went first.

"Can you describe Toe Taggin' Attire for me, Mr. Gunthry?"

"It's an immaculate building with state-of-the-art everything. The basement was my favorite place to be. Aside from every staff and artist having their own room, there was a kitchen, three full bathrooms, a movie room, and a large conference room. Jerrod spared no expense when it came to Toe Taggin' Attire. If there isn't a million dollars put into Toe Taggin' Attire, it's close to it."

"You testified that they never spoke about drug deals outside of the conference room."

"Never."

"They never did, or you never testified to that?" she asked.

"They never did."

"Okay. Can you describe the conference room for me please?"

"No one knew, but me and Jerrod, that the conference room was a room inside of ah room. The conference room itself was separated from the walls. We had it designed like that so that no word could leave the room, except from someone's mouth."

"What happened when Detective Jarvos sent you in with a wire?"

"I pulled Wild Bill in the conference room and told him that I heard a member from Slaughtermore Records had placed twenty-thousand dollars on his head."

"Can you clarify the term 'on his head'?"

"It's a kill contract. Termination."

"You may continue."

"Anyway, he laughed at me and said he wasn't worried, he knew no one inside of Slaughtermore had access to twenty thousand. I left out. When I met up with Detective Jarvos he took the wire off and all he heard was noise. He thought that the wire was messed up. After trying three different wires, I found out that conversations inside the conference room were protected by white noise generators. It made sense to me because I know how important electronics was to Jerrod."

"Why would anyone need a white-noise—"

"Objection, as to speculation," the prosecutor said.

"Sustained."

"Why do you think it was installed?"

"Like I said, everything went down in the conference room. Jerrod, Magik, 4Hunnid, Madd Lou, and Wild Bill had a meeting once a week like clock work. L-Trigga, Nyse, and DY showed up once a month for those meetings."

"Was there anyone else at those meetings?"

"Yeah, the money lady; Amil. She was always there. Anything that had to do with money, she was there," he told. "She use to have a saying which was also an anagram for her name 'All Money Is Legel'. She meant that."

Amil looked at Tommy Gunz in disbelief. She heard how Toe Taggin' always rapped about loyalty and keeping it four hunnid and not snitching, but she had never experienced being a victim of it. It disgusted her. She wanted to hurl insults at the pussy-nigga who sat before her. She wanted to take her seven-inch Louboutin's heels off and strike him repeatedly, and her face conveyed her thoughts. Margret Meed had to squeeze her knee to bring her back to reality. She mouthed the words 'Bitch-Ass Nigga' to him, not caring that the jury saw her. Margret popped her leg this time.

"Would you consider Toe Taggin' Posse Music Group dangerous?"

"Thee absolute worst. We are talking about niggas with songs like; Clap Yo' Motha, Steel Ya Breath, and Machine Gun Rap, and they meant every lyric they rap. But even that wasn't enough. Magik, Madd Lou,

L-Trigga, 4Hunnid, Wild Bill, Nyse, and DY formed their own faction called the Illuminati."

"What is the Illuminati?"

"Three beasts the city would never want to see come together; Bloods, Pirus, and BGF."

A silent hush went over the courtroom as they imagined the three-headed beast roaming the city's streets. Even Prosecutor Scott knew the weight of Tommy Gunz accusations. He knew the city controlled those organizations by separation. Together, all in one, was something that was never even visualized.

The judge regretted letting the reporters and their cameras in. He knew he'd be the reason, if this Illuminati business caught fire.

"Nothing further," she said, and sat down.

Rosenburg stood up. "I'm not going to be long. These meetings you say my client attended every week; these drug business meetings. Have you ever sat in on one of these meetings?"

"No."

"So, for all you know, they could've been discussing cake recipes? Cars? Music? Clothing? Women?"

(Chuckling) "Then why wasn't I allowed in?"

"I'm not sure Mr. Gunthry. Have you ever seen my client, Trayvon Cox, sell any kind of drug?"

"I didn't have to. I saw the Versace duffle bag filled to capacity with every dead president that ever lived."

"But you never saw him sell drugs?"

"No, but—"

"Nothing further Your Honor."

"Mr. Ravenel, you've not said one word since the trial began. Are you okay?"

"Yes, Your Honor. It's not my time yet."

"As you wish," the judge said.

Marget Meed got up and questioned him. She was a pitbull in a skirt too; just like her client.

Teresa, Connie Y's secretary, came in the courtroom, tiptoed over to the defense table, whispered something in Connie Y's ear, handed her a piece of paper, and scurried back out.

Connie Y watched as Margret Meed tore into him making him out of a liar in less than a half hour. When she was done, Connie Y stood up.

"How are you doing, Mr. Gunthry?"

"Connie Y," he said.

"Why are you here today?"

"To testify?"

"But why?"

(Sighing) "It's the right thing to do."

It was her turn to chuckle. "How long have you been a CI (Confidential Informant)?"

"I think it was January tenth, twenty thirteen. It was a Friday."

"January eleventh, it was. I've checked in to your bank account, and every first of the month, like clock work, since January eleventh you've been receiving two thousand, seven hundred dollars, from the state. Are you employed by the state?"

"Sorta."

"What do you mean by, sorta?"

"I said sorta, as in kinda. I get paid for telling."

"So your testimony is worth two thousand dollars?"

"Not really."

"Are you getting anything in return for your cooperation, besides two thousand and seven hundred dollars?"

"Nope."

Connie Y looked down at a piece of paper that she was holding, and then looked up to him.

"You sure? We already had one person to spend a few nights in jail for blatantly lying on the stand."

He thought about it in his head. A few days ain't shit he though. "Nope. I'm not getting anything in return for my cooperation."

"Mr. Gunthry, the reason why you said January tenth is the day you signed on to be a CI, instead of the eleventh; the actual day you signed on was because on January tenth, twenty thirteen, you were arrested with two packages of cocaine. One had seven hundred and forty point one grams in it, and the other held nine hundred and fifty-six point eight grams in it. Along with the two packages, police also found two AR 15s, and three digital scales. What baffles me is, these charges are no longer on your record, nor can I find a disposition. Would you please enlighten us on what happened to those charges?"

"I—"

"Keep in mind that you already lied once, Mr. Gunthery. Don't dig a deeper hole," Connie Y warned.

"The charges were dropped, due to lack of evidence," he said.

Connie Y burst into laughter.

"You find his answer amusing, Ms. Yaroborugh?"

"Yes, Your Honor," she said, handing the bailiff the paper she held in her hand. He gave it to the judge, the judge read it, and shook his head.

"Approach," he said. "The both of you."

Prosecutor Scott and Connie Y approached the bench.

"You, this is not a comedy club. This is a trial, where lives are on the line. So you better act like it, before it be you in a cell for contempt. And you, you shouldn't be so cocky. Your witnesses are screwing things up for you. I'm sending this idiot to jail too. You need to better prepare your witnesses."

"Yes, Your Honor, but I only have one more witness left, and I'll rest."

"Good," the judge said. "Did I make myself clear Ms. Yarborough?"

"Yes, sir Your Honor."

They both went back to where they were.

"Mr. Gunthry, all of the things that you were arrested for was in your possession; inside your car, making it an open and shut case—"

"Objection, Your Honor! Speculation."

"Sustained."

"Like I said, it was an open and shut case. Did the state offer to drop the charges for your cooperation?"

"Sorta."

"Explain yourself Mr. Gunthry."

"An addition to my cooperation, I had to try to get an undercover officer signed to Toe Taggin' Posse Music Group."

"Did you succeed?"

Tommy Gunz cracked a big smile, looked at 4Hunnid and said, "Let's just say, the debt that I owed the state, was paid in full."

"Let's break for lunch," Judge Gibson said.

***

4Hunnid punched the bullpen's wall until his knuckles bled. There was nothing none of his co-d's could say to make him feel any better about Azarah's betrayal. They just let him vent. Connie Y showed up immediately, out of breath. When the CO let her in she seen her nephew pacing the floor with blood dripping from his hands.

"Get me something to clean his hands, please," she told the CO. The rest of them walked over to Connie Y, while he paced. "I swear I didn't know they was putting her on the stand, nor did I know she was a cop."

Jerrod stepped up. "We know. How much damage can she do?"

"Yeah, 'cause we was looking good up until this shit," Wild Bill said.

"I'm not sure. You all should know better than me. I do know she was at the hospital with him after the kidnapping."

"Man, this could be the end of us," Wild Bill said.

"Everyone calm down. No one is going to jail. I don't give ah fuck if they dig up Speedy, Rick Flare, or BK, and put'em on the stand. We gon' be aiight," Magik said. "Who you puttin' on the stand once they finished?"

"The waitress from Kobe's."

"You want to win this case Connie Y?" Magik asked.

"Yes."

"Well, let Cardeen take the lead."

"What?"

"Let Cardeen call the first witness," he said, seriously. "Look, you said you want to win, right? So listen to me. After Cardeen finish, the case will be over. Just trust me. Can you do that?"

"I don't know Magik. At the sake of my nephew? I don't know about that, and Cardeen is known for being a trickster in the courtroom."

"Which is why I hired him for Trina. Just trust me."

"King Davenport, come here," Connie Y said.

He walked over to them. "What?"

"Magik wants me to let Cardeen go first. Are you—"

"I don't care what you do. Get this shit over."

"Let me talk to him y'all," she said. They all walked over to the corner, at the same time, the CO passed her some baby wipes and napkins through the bars. "Come here boy. Let me see you hands. What have you done to yourself?" she asked, when he stuck his hands through the bars. "You've allowed this girl to mess with you mentally."

"No."

She raised his hands a little, causing him to winced a little. "I can't tell. When she takes the stand, we cannot afford to let the jurors see any emotions from you. Now, I'm going to ask you again. Should I allow Cardeen to take the lead?"

"Let'em. I trust Magik with my life."

"But everyone says he's been acting weird. Your life is on the line, his isn't."

"Which is why I know he knows something we don't. Let'em."

"Listen King, I know he's your childhood friend. I know you love him unconditionally. And you trust him, but this is a death penalty case. Which means, if you are found guilty, I will be fighting to get you life in prison. LIFE!" she screamed. "Now you listen to—"

"No, you listen to me, Aunt C. I'm not tryna die no quicker than the next man, but if it's my time; fuck it. I lived a helluva life. I've accomplished a lot. Trust me Aunt C, I'm good whichever way it goes. You wanna know why gangstas can live with any hand they're dealt?"

"Why?" she asked, with tears in her eyes.

"Simply because the life we lived, wasn't a lie. We stand ten toes down all the time, at all times."

"But—"

"No buts. Let Cardeen do whatever he gon' do."

She nodded her head and left.

4Hunnid walked over to Magik.

"You good bruh?" Magik asked.

"Hell nah bruh, but um wit'chu. Whatever you got going on, I hope it works."

"We good, trust me." Magik assured his best friend.

***

Connie Y went in the bathroom and cried like a baby. Kia came looking for her ten minutes later.

"Connie, you in here?"

"Yes."

"Come on, some major shit going on out here," she said. Connie Y walked out of the stall. One look at her and Kia knew. "Awww shit. Come here girl," she said, holding her arms out. "I know you're worried about your nephew, but girl let me tell you, I've been representing Tree Top ever since I became a lawyer, and trust me, they always find a way to come out on top. Them motherfuckers are like cats. They got nine lives," she said, causing Connie Y to laugh. "Now get yourself together so we can go up here and finish fighting these white folks."

***

Defense Lawyor'a Conforonoc Room...

Connie Y was the last one to walk in the room. Everyone was talking amongst themselves, but stopped once Connie Y cleared her throat.

"Listen up, I—"

"Before you begin Connie, let me say this," Margret Meed interrupted. "I do not believe the state satisfied the court with their case against my client, so I'll be filing a motion to dismiss all charges against her for lack of evidence. The only way I won't do it, is if this girl get up on the stand and say something so drastic against my client, that I have no choice but to cross examine her. Other than that, I'm filing. I just didn't want anyone surprised when we get upstairs."

"I respect that. Anyone else?"

"Yes. I'll be adopting that motion. I don't believe they made a case against my client either," Ivan Bates said. "I want Cardeen to do the same. They haven't proved their case against Katrina either."

All eyes went on Howard Cardeen.

"Although I agree with you, Bates, I'm not. It's imperative that my client remain on this case, to ensure that no one gets the death penalty, and everyone goes home."

"Speaking of which, I was instructed to let Cardeen lead the pack. So when the state rest their case, it's your show Cardeen."

"Thank you. We'll all be filing dismissal motions," he smiled, wickedly. "Trust me," he said, but the other lawyers were skeptical.

They didn't trust Cardeen at all.

CHAPTER 28
Toe Tagging's Pussy

The courtroom was a mist of murmurs until the bailiff came in and announced the emergence of the judge. He told everyone to be seated and reminded everyone of his strict courtroom rules. He told them to use the two individuals he had arrested for perjury as an example.

"State, you may continue with your case."

"Thank you, Your Honor," Prosecutor Scott said, and called his next witness.

Everyone in the courtroom was shocked silent. The witness was sworn in.

"State, your name for the record, please."

"Officer Kevin Thomas."

"What did the defendants know you as?"

"I was introduced to them as Denni Man, but Jerrod quickly changed my name to Train."

"What was your role in Toe Tagging Posse Music Group?"

"I was an artist."

"How did you become and artist?"

"Thomas 'Tommy Gunz' Gunthry introduced me to Jerrod. I freestyled for him, and he signed me on the spot."

"Did you undergo a background check?"

"I'm sure I did. Jerrod does background checks on everyone that he employs. He's skeptical and do not trust anyone but his four homies; 4Hunnid, Madd Lou, Magik, and Wild Bill. He never trusted me at all and it showed in how he treated me."

"How did the rest of the artist treat you?"

"All but one treated me like a brother."

"All but one?"

"Yes. There is a female that's signed to Toe Taggin' Posse too. She's the first lady. Her name Queen Azarah. She hated my guts and told me so, plenty of times. She even ran in my room at Toe Taggin' Attire and put a gun in my mouth."

Prosecutor Scott was pissed off that he mentioned her name after he specifically told him not to. Kevin Thomas was stepping on his chances of becoming the next head prosecutor.

"How much time would you say you've spent with the Toe Tagging Posse Music Group artists?"

"Every day for the past year and a half. I was committedly with them. I had a job to do."

"And what job was that?"

"To investigate and gather information on the most violent rap crew in Baltimore City."

"Why do you call them the most violent?" Scott asked.

"Why? Because I've witnessed them in action."

"Can you tell the courts some of the things you've witnessed undercover?"

"Yes. Like one time we were performing at Ram's Head Live. One guy was in the front of the stage with his arms folded and a scowl on his face. He stood out because everyone else around him was dancing and having fun. I knew it was going to be trouble, so I prayed the man left before our set was over. That was not to be the case. 4Hunnid, Madd Lou, and Wild Bill ended up beating that guy up real bad. I recently went to the guy's house to talk to him about testifying, but he was scared of retaliation. He said he knew all too well about the gang's reach, and he wanted no parts of it "

"Another incident that stood out to me is the time we went to the Blammy Awards at 5 Seasons. It was a big night for us, because we were being nominated in sixteen of the twenty-two categories. It wasn't enough to take home thirteen of the sixteen awards. Wild Bill saw a fan from Slaughtermore Records wearing a 'F' Toe Taggin' Posse shirt. When they caught the fan outside, they all beat him with GTV vodka bottles until he was unconscious."

"Yes, that's violent. Going in, what questions were you looking to answer?"

"Off top, how were they living in lavish luxury. And I'm not talking about ghetto, hood luxury, where five or six pairs of two hundred dollar jeans, a couple pairs Louis Vuitton shoes, and some Gucci shoes made you rich. Every person of Toe Taggin' Posse was rich. They dressed rich, they were rich. I wanted to know how, because rapping doesn't put six hundred thousand in your bank account, unless you are a famous rapper, such as Drake, Little Wayne, or Rick Ross an even they have ventures outside of rapping."

"And what did you find out?"

"It was heroin. Heroin made them rich."

"So it was heroin that made them rich?"

"Heroin made them rich, but how they sold it made them almost untouchable."

"What do you mean?"

"They didn't sell heroin like everyone else. There were no touters yelling the name of the product on their corners. There were no large crowds on the block. Most surprisingly, not one member owned a phone. In the year and a half that I was with them, I've never seen them use a phone."

"So how did they conduct business?"

"Through Amil. She ripped and ran for them. All over the city. Wherever she had to go, she went, with no question. That's how messages were passed throughout the city."

"How often were you at Toe Taggin' Attire?"

"A lot. Most of my time was spent at the store?"

"Have you ever seen anyone, other than a clothing customer, outside of Toe Tagging Posse Music Group, inside of the store?"

"No. They were pretty low key with their drug dealing business. They talked about and did their business in The Dungeon's conference room, which was special in itself, from what I was told."

"What were you told, and by who?"

"I was told by my confidential informant, Thomas 'Tommy Gunz' Gunthry, that conversations cannot be recorded inside of the conference room, due to some devices Jerrod had installed inside. Of course, I tried it for myself. It was true. All I heard on the recordings were white noise, and a whole bunch of chatter, like in a crowded bar."

"Were you ever present inside of the conference room while drug business was being discussed?"

"No. No one was ever allowed inside at their meetings but, Amil, Jerrod, 4Hunnid, Wild Bill, Madd Lou, Magik, L-Trigga, Nyse and DY. Those were the only ones of the crew who were involved in the drug trade."

"Was Toe Tagging Attire a front for money laundering?" Scott asked.

"I thought so nt first, but Too Taggin' Attire is a legitimate business, with a legitimate product, that's legitimately being sold. Dee Dee has her faults, but she ran that store right and she made a lot of money selling Toe Taggin' Posse Music Group attire."

"What did you mean by Dee Dee has her faults? Who is Dee Dee?"

"Dee Dee aka Antionette Brown, confided in me a month ago, and told me and I quote "Something is up with this bitch and if I find out she got anything to do with them being locked up, I'll kill her." She was referring to Queen Azarah, the female member of the group. See, Dee Dee thought that Azarah was the informant that helped put these guys behind bars. I couldn't have her running around seeking answers, so I had her arrested. Azarah has since gone missing, but she claims she knows nothing. That's what I meant by she has her faults. She is the store's owner."

Prosecutor Criag Scott questioned him for three hours, finally giving the defense a crack at him at five pm. Instead of cross examining him, the defense asked for a recess until the next day. The judge granted their request.

***

Steel Side (N-Section)...

Madd Lou was on the top bunk smoking an overstuffed cigarillo when 4Hunnid came in with his shower stuff and towel wrapped around his dreads.

He passed the cigarillo to him.

"What you thinking about 4Hunnid?"

"Nothing bruh."

"Come on bruh. I know you like I know myself. I know when something on ya mind. What is it?"

4Hunnid broke down. Madd Lou had to get up and jumped down to make sure he wasn't hearing things.

"You cryin' an' shit bruh," he laughed.

"This bitch was up under us the whole time. A fuckin' police. I wanna kill this bitch so bad," the anger inside of him dripped with every word he spoke. "This shit got me mad as ah bitch. You see how that nigga looked at us and laughed when he walked out the courtroom? The only reason I ain't get up and grab his neck was because Connie Y was blocking me. He gotta go before I go. That's on Tree Top, his ass going before me."

"You want me to place the order?"

"Naw, I got it. I got a feeling the order has already been placed," he smiled.

***

O-Section...

"You think Bates gon' get you off?" L-Trigga asked, as he passed the blunt to DY.

"I 'on't know. I hope he do. The state's case was weak as shit. I thought they were gonna have ah open and shut case. They don't have no controlled buys, no pictures, or no phone calls. All they got is some fuckin' fiends. Shouldn't nobody go to jail."

"I agree. Even their surprise witnesses was bullshit. I know for a fact their death penalty case dead. They can't kill no one off this weak shit."

A CO walked in front of their cell. DY tried his best to hide the blunt, but the smoke coming from his mouth was betraying him.

"Boy, I know y'all smoking. You can smell that shit in the hallway," she said.

"What's up G?"

"What's up with you Trigga?" G asked. "How you holding up baby?"

"Shit, you know me. I'm good."

"That's fucked up about that nigga Train. He's a real bitch-ass nigga. They started a YouTube page in his honor. Every video is letting the world know how much they hate him. They using his cds as a toilet, a Frisbee, a door stopper, and a bunch of other shit. They burning his clothes. The video that got over three million views was the one y'all homegirl, Tiffeny, made. She went down to the edge of Interstate 83 and gave one of Train's shirts to a homeless man. The homeless man took one look at it, and went off. He wiped his ass with it and everything. Then Tiffeny went to the store, grabbed all of the shirts with his face on it, took them out back and set them on fire."

"That's good."

"I came up here because I got some information for you. I'm ready to prove my loyalty to you and the Illuminati."

"And how you gonna do that?" L-Trigga asked.

"They got me working on 'B' section. Toe Taggin's A&R is being housed over there."

Both, DY and L-Trigga jumped up at the news.

"Tommy Gunz is in this jail?"

"I just said that, DY," she laughed.

"Wait, 'B' section is down by Receiving. How is we gon' get over there and back without getting caught?"

"I didn't say it was a cake-walk baby. He's down there in the last cell on the west side. I'm down there. I'll open his door; the rest is up to y'all."

"You know this means your job, and ah investigation, and at the most; jail time," L-Trigga warned.

"I said I was ready to prove my loyalty. Besides, that secretary/assistant position is still open at Kode of Silence, right?"

"You damn right it is."

"So make it happen then. I'll be there," she said, and walked off.

"That nigga gotta go," L-Trigga said.

"Shit, he gone already," DY said, and yelled out the cell to one of his comrades.

"What's up Yummy?"

"The two brothers that just got the three life sentences, what section they on?"

"They on 'C' section."

"Good, good. I need to get a kite down there to them. I need it read to them, and destroyed afterwards."

"No problem. Put it together, and I'll make it happen."

***

177

Receiving...

The COs working Receiving was playing UNO when they heard a loud scream come from 'C' section. They ran down to see what was going on. Four bloodied inmates were standing at the gate. The receiving officer hit the code and COs came from everywhere, running. 'D' section grill was left wide open. The hallman for Receiving waited until all the COs had disappeared on 'C' section before he ran on 'B' section. The lockbox was left open with the key inside. He hit the lever to open the last cell on the west side.

When he made it to the cell, Tommy Gunz was laying in the bed reading, with his head facing the grill.

"What'chu came to give me some ass, Ms. G?"

"Naw, I came to send you to hell, you rat-ass nigga."

Tommy Gunz couldn't move quick enough. The guy pulled out a flip-out knife and stabbed him in his head. It got stuck, so he pulled out another one and stabbed him over seventy-five times. He wrote a message on the wall in Tommy Gunz' blood. Once he was done, he cleaned the handle of the embedded knife, and stuck something in the grill, to make it look like Tommy Gunz tricked his door and left out. Ms. G met him on the way out with a change of clothes, and a lot of towels. She locked the lock box and went back around to 'C' section, but not before locking the hallman in one of Receiving's bullpens.

***

8:00 a.m. (Courtroom)...

They went through the ritual of Judge Gibson's courtroom and then something out of the ordinary happened. The judge excused the jury to the breakroom, told the media to leave out, and cleared out the spectator's seats inside the courtroom. The judge, the prosecutor, the bailiff, the judge's secretary, the CO escorts, the defendants, and their attorneys were the only people still inside the courtroom.

"Prosecutor Scott, you have the floor."

Scott stood up with a newspaper in his hand.

"Breaking News," he read. "Last night, a correctional officer found Thomas Gunthry aka Tommy Gunz, former A&R and recently exposed confidential informant, choking on his own blood. Gunthry was found on the floor of his bloody cell. He was pronounced dead a few minutes after he was found."

"Authorities are left with the task of finding out how was it that someone was able to get to him on the secure protective custody unit." He put the paper down. "This paper doesn't halfway describe what I saw when I went to the jail last night. It was a brutal massacre. Mr. Gunthry was stabbed seventy-seven times, and was found with a six-inch knife embedded in his head. On the wall, in the cell was a clear indication message of who was responsible. It said: *LOOSE LIPS SINKS LEGENDS 4XL Illuminati.*"

"Your Honor, what does this has to do with the defendants sitting here today? These defendants were securely locked in their cells at the time of the murder," Connie Y said.

"I agree," Kia Perry said, "Not one defendant admitted to being apart of this made-up faction that Gunthry dubbed Illuminati. They shouldn't be held accountable for it."

"Do you have anything else to say Mr. Scott?"

(Sighing) "No, Your Honor."

"Bring everyone back in bailiff."

"What was that about?" 4Hunnid whispered to his aunt.

"A scare tactic. He's getting nervous."

The judge reminded everyone of his courtroom rules before he turned it over to the defense.

"Defense."

Connie Y stood up. She shocked everyone in the courtroom, except for the lawyers and clients, by saying:

"Nothing further Your Honor."

Everyone just knew the defense was waiting to sink their teeth in the undercover officer. They "knew" wrong. The defense had a plan. No one knew what that plan was, besides Howard Cardeen, but they were putting their trust in him.

"State?" Judge Gibson said.

"The state rests."

"Defense."

"Your Honor, I'd like to file a motion," Margret Meed said.

The judge dismissed the jury again.

"Yes, Ms. Meed."

"I move to file a motion to dismiss all charges against my client. Prosecutor Scott skated around my client the whole time. He didn't prove money laundering, fraud, or conspiracy. Money laundering or fraud wasn't mentioned until now."

"State, your rebuttal."

"None Your Honor."

"Your motion is granted. All charges against Ms. DeCario is hereby dismissed," Judge Gibson said. "Anyone else?"

"I move to adopt Meed's motion, Your Honor," Ivan Bates said.

"State, your rebuttal."

Prosecutor Scott stood up and went in for thirty minutes on why he felt like he proved his case against DY.

"Motion denied. Would anyone else like to be heard?"

No one spoke, so he sent for the jury. When they came back in, he explained to them why Amil was no longer amongst the accused. He looked at Connie Y and said, "Defense."

Connie Y looked at 4Hunnid, who nodded his head slightly. She then looked down to Howard Cardeen. He stood up, smoothed his suit down with his hands and cleared his throat. "Your Honor, I'd like to recall a state witness," he said, in a bold move.

"Excuse me?"

"A state witness, sir."

Prosecutor Scott sat up in his chair wondering what type of fuckery was Cardeen pulling. He knew Cardeen very well.

"As you wish."

"The defense would like to recall Detective Talia Coppola."

Scott looked at Cardeen, who gave him an award-winning smile. She walked in the courtroom with every eye on her or her derriere, and took the stand. Scott was so nervous, he asked to approach the bench. The judge allowed Cardeen, Connie Y, and Scott to approach.

"Your Honor, Ms. Yarborough is the lead. If Cardeen is leading, then it can only mean one thing; tricks."

"Fight the case Scott. I'm well aware of Mr. Cardeen's courtroom antics, and we've already spoken."

"Thank you, Your Honor," Cardeen said, as the judge dismissed them. "How are you doing detective?"

"Fine, sir."

"Okay, let's get to it. You testified early on that you've arrested Mr. Davenport three times for disorderly conduct. Is that correct, detective?"

"Yes. It is."

"What was the nature of the arrest?"

"It was mainly his lewd, inappropriate comments to me, and his gestures," she said.

"What did he say, if you can remember?"

She looked around nervously.

"We're all grown in here, detective," Cardeen said.

"Objection, Your Honor—"

"Is this necessary Mr. Cardeen?"

"Yes, Your Honor."

"Sustained, you may answer the question, Detective Coppola."

"He used to grab his private area, and tell me how thick he thought I was. He called me the 'b' word a few times."

"How did that make you feel?" Cardeen asked.

"Like any woman, I felt disrespected. Mr. Davenport is a very rude and disrespectful person."

"Have you ever arrested anyone else from Toe Taggin' Posse Music Group or affiliates with them for similar disrespect."

"Yes, I've arrested Deyont☐ Harvey before too."

"For what?"

"With Deyont☐ Harvey, it's different. He has his own language of sorts. Like, everything he says to you is a verse or a lyric from a song. So most of the things he has said to me, went over my head or was so well hidden, I didn't realize I was being disrespected."

"On the day I arrested him, he said something to the effect of 'come here with your dumb ass'. I've heard him use that term on his fans, and them use it back, so I wasn't offended, but later on that night he grabbed my hand, and tried to touch my behind. I arrested him immediately."

"You felt disrespected, detective?"

"Very much," she said.

"Have you ever disrespected any of the defendants?"

"No. Never."

"How about yourself? You ever disrespect yourself?"

"Objection," Scott yelled.

"No need. I'm done with her Your Honor."

"You may step down detective."

"What do you mean by that? No, I've never disrespected myself."

"You didn't have to answer that detective. You may step down," Judge Gibson said.

She stepped down, eyeing Howard Cardeen. He winked at her.

"I would like to call Katrina Clayborne to the stand."

Katrina made her way to the stand, got sworn in, and took a seat.

"Ms. Clayborne, how long have you been an affiliate of Toe Taggin' Posse Music Group?"

"Since its inception."

"How so?"

"I'm the girlfriend of that fine brother over there."

"Let the record reflect that she's referring to Arlando Gilyard," he said. "How long have you two been together?"

"We met in middle school. We fell in love in high school and I've been his ever since."

"How would you describe your relationship?"

"Like any other young love; rough around the edges, but we are in love," she said, with love written all over her pretty face.

"You ever have problems with infidelity?"

"Not at all."

"Come on. Mr. Gilyard is young, handsome, successful, wealthy, and not to mention he's in the entertainment business. You mean to tell me, you've never, ever, had a problem with him being unfaithful?"

"Never, not once."

"So he's never had sex outside of you two's relationship, since high school?"

"I never said that," she corrected him.

"Okay, lets change directions for a second. How well do you know Mr. Gilyard?"

"Like I know myself."

"Permission to do an in-court demonstration, Your Honor?"

"Oh boy," Prosecutor Scott said. He was already accustomed to Cardeen's antics. He knew Cardeen was the type of lawyer who liked to entertain the jurors, keep them awake, as well as keep them on the edge of their chairs. Cardeen's tactics were something of a magician's. He'd lure you in with the trick, the whole time, making you forget about the matter at hand, diverting your attention. It wasn't to be that way though. Judge Gibson put an end to it before it had even begun, by denying him permission.

"Okay, gotta keep it simple," he said, getting some laughs out of the jurors. "Let's try this. You've seen your significant other grow as a person, haven't you?"

That was leading but Scott stayed quiet. He didn't want to give him any more ammo. He seen that the jurors were loving Cardeen.

"Of course. He has come a long way. I tell him that all the time. I'm very proud of him."

"What would you say his proudest moment was?"

"Objection, as to Ms. Clayborne knowing what Mr. Gilyard's proudest moment was."

"Your Honor, I intended to prove just how well my client knows her other half with my demonstration, but, since I didn't have permission, I'll just rely on the fact that they've been together since the age of twelve."

"Overruled. You may answer the question," the judge said.

"I would say his proudest moment was being apart of history. The day that Toe Taggin' Posse Music Group sold out the Baltimore Arena."

"Were you present that day?" Cardeen asked her.

"I sure was."

"Was there an afterparty afterwards?"

"Yes, there was."

"Where was it, If you can recall?"

"It was at the Normandy Room, on January 18th, 2014."

"It must've been a very special day, for you to remember the date."

"It was a special day, umm," she said, remembering the day.

"Who, from your immediate circle attended the afterparty?"

"Everyone… except for me that is."

"You didn't attend the afterparty on this special night?"

"No. I had something better planned for my man."

"Oh really?"

"Really," she smiled.

"What did you do when you left the Baltimore Area?"

"I drove straight to the 4 Seasons hotel and purchased one of the presidential suites."

"I'm assuming you've had presidential suites before?"

"Of course. I've had them in at least twenty-four states," Trina said.

"So what made this one special?"

"My baby had been asking me lately to spice up our sex life, and being as though he deserved it, from his performance, I figured it was now or never. So I set up a night he wouldn't forget, and just in case he did, I recorded the whole night."

Cardeen went to the table and picked up a plastic bag with a CD in it that was labeled Samantha's Sex Tape.

"Can you remind the court who Samantha is?"

"She's the first lady of a rival rap label of ours; Slaughtermore Records. She's also the ex-girlfriend of Traum, aka Lawrence Weathers, and the current girlfriend of his brother; Looney Redz aka Leonard Weathers."

"And what is on this CD?"

"A homemade sex tape of us gettin' it in."

"Us, as in who?"

"Me, Samantha, and Magik."

"A threesome?"

"Yes."

"Is that what you had planned for Mr. Gilyard on January the 18th of this year?"

"Yes, but it was more special on that day."

"Let's see. Ladies and gentlemen, we are all adults here. This disc I am about to play is a graphic one."

"Objection, Your Honor as—"

"Overruled, you may—"

"Can we approach?" Prosecutor Scott asked.

"Sure," the judge said, tired of Scott's incompetence.

Connie Y, Cardeen, and Scott approached the judge's bench.

"Your Honor, is this really necessary? We all know what's on the disc?"

"Do you really know what's on the disc, Prosecutor Scott?"

"I do, and no one wants to see the naked bodies, and sexual acts of the accused."

The judge shook his head. "Did you even prepare for this case Mr. Scott? Or did you walk in my courtroom unprepared, with the attitude of having an open and shut case?" His face gave the judge his answer. "You should be ashamed of yourself. I've been over every piece of evidence submitted in this case, in its entirety, and I assure you – you are not even close to an open and shut case. Now, I'm going to allow this video to be shown, because I know you haven't seen it. Had you did, you wouldn't be in front of me now with that silly look on your face, wasting my and the tax payers time and money. Now sit down and enjoy the show."

Connie Y felt a little ashamed herself, because she herself had failed to watch the whole disc. She didn't want to see two kids, that she considered her own, have sex.

The judge instructed the media to turn their cameras off, and everyone to turn their phones off. He then told the bailiff to confiscate any device that was recording.

Cardeen played the video.

The first scene that was displayed was Samantha on her back, with Trina riding her face with her arms wrapped around Samantha's legs, while Magik was slamming hisself inside of her. Most eyes were on the video, a few were on Trina, and some were on Magik.

The moans and groans from the video was a bit much and caused a lot of people to squirm in their seats, or adjust their crotches or panties. That scene faded out and another one came on. This one was inside a plush hotel room. Trina was seen setting the room up in a robe and footie socks. She looked to be moving in a hurry.

"Where the hell is room service?" they heard her say, as they watched her light the scented candles.

She placed a bowl of diced pineapples inside of the refrigerator, then she moved the camera to where it was facing the bed.

They heard a knock at the door.

"You gonna let me in? Hurry up 'fore someone sees me," they heard a woman say.

"Ain't nobody gonna see you. Come on in?"

When both women came into the view of the camera, all who didn't know, made some involuntary noise, causing Judge Gibson to bang his gavel, and scream, "ORDER IN THE COURT!"

The two women engaged in sexual acts until Magik walked in the room thirty minutes later. He caught his woman, Trina, on her back and another woman deep sea diving between her legs.

"Come on baby, you got your chocolate pussy to play with and some new vanilla pussy. Come dig in." Trina said.

Everyone watched the monitor for the next forty-five minutes as Trina, Magik, and Detective Talia Coppola have the best sex of their lives. Coppola was so wantonly engaged in the threeway copulation, that she was unaware of the words that Magik had her repeating. Those words were the daggers in the state's case.

"I'll do anything for you!"

"Yes, I'll do anything!"

"Yes, Toe Taggin' Posse forever!"

"Fuck, ugh, ooh, the police!"

Prosecutor Scott's face turned fifty shades of red as he listened to an officer say all types of raunchy things in the heat of passion. He wanted to cry. He realized the case was beyond his grasp. It was forty-five minutes before the video was over.

Cardeen stood up.

"Your Honor. I'm finish with this witness."

"State."

"No, Your Honor. I have nothing."

"You may step down."

She stepped down and winked at Magik, who smiled back.

"I would like to recall Detective Talia—"

"Your Honor. Can we approach?"

"Yes. Approach."

Connie Y, Cardeen, and Prosecutor Scott approached once again.

"Yes, Mr. Scott."

"There's no need to recall the detective up. We get that point. There's no need to embarrass her more."

"I believe she initiated the embarrassment."

"I agree, but there's no need to continue down this road."

"Your Honor, this case has been compromised by a lead detective. We are all filing motions to dismiss on the count of investigative misconduct," Cardeen said.

"I will allow you to file motions, but I will sleep on it, and rule on it in the morning. Let's adjourn for the rest of the day. It's been a trying day," Judge Gibson said.

The judge dismissed everyone and allowed the nine lawyers to file their motions. The guys were transferred back to Steel Side. The lawyers dined at La Garage on West 36 Street and discussed today's trial.

"That was a good move Howard, but you should've consulted with us first," John Hassett said.

"I agree," Connie Y said. "Had you told us, we could've went about this a different way. This could still go bad for us."

They looked at Connie Y like she was crazy.

"She's right. Gibson can still rule the disc inadmissible on the grounds that she was unaware that she was being recorded. He can declare the mistrial, and then make us suite up for another trial," Kia Perry said.

"That was incredibly stupid of you Howard."

"Watch it Margret. I only did what my client instructed me to do... to the letter. I was paid in full, so I did what was asked of me."

"What's our chances Connie?" Ron Caroline asked.

"You never know with Gibson."

"She's right," Christine Needlemen said. "Gibson will give you the impression that he's on your side, then he'll stick the dagger in you."

"Fuck!" Rosenberg exclaimed. "Our reputations are on the line here. Why didn't you just consult with us? We're a team Cardeen."

"Let's not fall apart here, guys," Ivan Bates said.

"Ivan's right," Ravenell said. "We still have a case to fight. Let's lay it all on the table now. What do we have Connie?"

"Worst case? He rules the disc inadmissible, declares a mistrial and we repack a jury. We do know no one's getting the death penalty. Their case is very weak. We can take them on again. The question is, will Scott be willing to go to trial again."

"Scott is a pussy. He won't want another trial. Too much public humiliation. He needed this case to secure his spot as Baltimore's new SA (State's Attorney)," Kia Perry said. "He'll want to move on the next high profile case to save face."

"That brings us to best case scenario. Gibson rules in our favor, and deems the disc admissible. All charges are dropped, all accounts are unfrozen, and all assets returned."

"Let's hope that new wife of Gibson's puts him in a good mood.

***

Judge Gibson's home...

It was three a.m. and Judge Gibson was still up reviewing the case. He didn't like the fact that Howard Cardeen had once again turned his courtroom into a circus. He felt like Cardeen had totally disregarded the conversation they had in his chambers.

His wife walked in his office, still wiping her eyes, in her underwear and housecoat.

"You're up honey?"

"I rolled over and didn't feel you there. I figured you were in here. The case isn't over yet?"

"No and my decision tomorrow will make it even longer," he said, and explained the situation to her. He knew she loved hearing about his cases.

"So you're not going to allow them to use the disc?"

"No."

She came around his side of the desk and took a seat in his lap, looking at the mounds of paper on his desk. She began picking up papers.

"What's this husband?"

"The mug shots of the ten accused. This is the one that was on the video with the detective."

"Umph," she said, staring at the other papers on the desk.

"What's on your mind, honey? I know when you have something on your mind. What is it?"

She let her robe fall to the floor. "You ever wanted to do something out of the ordinary at work?" she asked, pulling her bra straps down.

"What do you mean, Lisa?"

"I mean, you're predictable baby. I've heard you everyday complain about the fatuity of this idiotic prosecutor. Everyone is expecting you to rule in the favor of the prosecutor."

"And you think I shouldn't?"

"No, you shouldn't. Why should the people of Baltimore City have an imbecile for a States Attorney? We shouldn't suffer. You can stop him from getting that seat, honey."

"You sound very passionate about this."

She squirmed in his lap, causing his loins to stir. "Yes, I am passionate about it."

"So I should release these criminals to the streets?"

She kissed him.

"If…(muah) they…(muah) oooh…(muah) really… (muah) are… (muah) criminals… (muah) they'll… (muah) mess… (muah) up… (muah) again."

She removed her underwear and his pants and got on her knees.

"So... what's your ruling, Judge Gibson?" she asked, and went down on him.

"Ughhh," he said. He grabbed the back of her head and pushed her down further than she was going. He knew that made her hotter. She had him squirting down her throat in four minutes flat.

"Good God!" he said, breathlessly.

"Order in the court," she said, getting up. She turned around and allowed him to see her best asset. She bent over, looked through her own legs at him and asked,

"What's the verdict, Judge?"

"I'm going to grant the defense's motions."

She began shaking her derriere in excitement. "Now come put me back to bed."

CHAPTER 29
The Turning Point

Everybody was on the edge of their seats waiting for the judge to come in. The jury had not been summoned from the room because of the pending motions that was filed by the defense team.

Prosecutor Scott was distraught over his performance in the trial. He underestimated the criminals, even after reading the biography of a former Baltimore City police lieutenant who had investigated the gang in 2005. The one thing the lieutenant stressed throughout the book, was to never underestimate them, and he did.

The defendants all had butterflies in their stomachs. Wild Bill kept letting out little, ghastly, involuntary-farts, upsetting his lawyer. None of them knew what the future held, but it was good to know that the state's death penalty request was out of the window. By now, the whole city knew about Talia Coppola's threesome with Magik and Trina. She didn't give the department a chance to fire her. She resigned, embarrassingly.

Dee Dee was released the night before and was now sitting in the audience with a bunch of other spectators. Against the bailiff's wishes, when she came in, she spoke to each one of her boys, and Trina.

Also in the courtroom, was Mary Hanson (Rick Flare's mother), in support of her boy toy, Nyse. Taedo, Flee and Sos'a also showed up in support. Queen Azarah Williams on the other hand, was still MIA. There was no word at all on the songstress, 4Hunnid was worried that Looney Redz got a hold of her for payback.

***

"All rise," the bailiff said.

The judge came in, gave his normal speech and got down to business.

"Yesterday, the defense filed motions in my court and I've been over the evidence. The conduct and words of Detective Coppola is enough to do away with this case. I'm granting the motions. Case dismissed."

The courtroom erupted in cheers. The accused stood up and embraced each other. Nyse looked over at Prosecutor Scott and said, "Look at'cha dumbass boy!"

"Order in the court!" Judge Gibson yelled, banging his gavel. "Order in the court!'

***

Central Bookings Intake Center...
Correctional officers came from all over the building to see and congratulate the Toe Taggin' Posse, Nyse,

L-Trigga, and DY. Some staff even pulled out phones to take pictures with them.

They were processed out at eleven pm. When they walked out on Eager Street, it looked like a concert out there. Reporters, fans, fellow rappers, and scantily clad women were all over the place. Everyone was screaming their names loudly.

"Was'sup wit'chall dumbasses?"

"Was'sup wit'cha dumbass," they responded back to Nyse.

A stretch Benz truck drove down Eager Street slowly, through the throngs of people. The truck stopped in front of the Central Bookings' entrance. Trina popped up through the sunroof with the two sparkle-topped bottles of GTV liquor.

"Come on y'all, lets go!"

They partied all night, ending their night at Norma Jean's Strip Club.

***

Prince Fredrick Maryland...

Kevin Thomas grabbed one of the last moving boxes from his Duke Street home, that he shared with his wife, and kids. He loaded the box in his SUV and hustled back to the house for the last box. He grabbed the box up. He was on his way out the door when something froze him. He dropped the box and removed his department-issued Glock .40 from its holster, in the small of his back. Undercover Officer Kevin Thomas pointed the gun outward and looked around the empty house. He inhaled deeply, through his nostrils. There was no denying the sweet smell of that intoxicating perfume; Balenciaga L'Essence.

She was or is here, he thought as he moved around his house carefully.

The smell got stronger when he got to him and his wife's old bedroom. He turned the knob slowly and pushed the door open. He crept in with the gun leading the way. He saw something in the corner of the empty bedroom. He walked closer and saw the Balenciaga perfume bottle. As soon as he bent over to pick it up he heard a gun cock back.

"Slowly, and I do mean slowly, place the gun on the floor, next to the perfume." He hesitated. "Please don't try me Officer Thomas. You did your background check on me, so you know I train at the same cop gun range as you. You may have even saw my competition posters hanging up in Bob's office."

"Why are you doing this?" he asked.

"I'll tell you once you put the gun down. I'm not asking again."

"Come on Azarah—"

"Engage the suspect in conversation. Keep them talking. Wait until they slip, and then make your move. Make it count," she said, quoting the officer's manual. "I know the book cover to cover, Thomas. Drop it, or I'll kill you, then make the call to 4Hunnid to kill your kids, and pretty wife out there in Oakland, Maryland."

He dropped the gun immediately and stood up to face her.

"Why are you doing this? We are in the same boat. They find out who you are, and you're a dead woman too."

"You can never compare me to you. I'm nothing like you. I'll never get on the stand on nobody. I'm no snitch. You are a bitch. Them niggas took you in like family."

He looked at the silencer on her gun and sighed. "You don't have to do this Azarah. Think about it. You are about to kill a cop. A fucking cop."

"Wrong. I'm killing a snake. A rat," she smiled. "A pig."

Choof. Choof. Choof. Choof. Choof. Choof.

She walked over to his body and fired four more shots in his head.

Choof. Choof. Choof. Choof.

She went in his pockets, picked up the Balenciaga bottle, and made her escape.

***

4Hunnid's House…

He was laying in his bed, smoking a blunt of Cali Dro when Azarah walked in.

"Where's Two T's?"

4Hunnid sat up, in his boxers and just looked at her.

"What?" she asked.

"You been MIA for all this time, and the only thing you gotta say is where's Two T's?"

"I was with you in spirit, bae."

He got off the bed and searched her. She raised her arms to assist him.

"Still don't trust me, huh?"

"I did, until now."

"Liar!" she screamed, as he removed and checked her clothes. "You were expecting me to walk in there and testify on you, wasn't you?"

"Naw."

"Liar!" she screamed. "I watched the whole trial on TV. I saw your face everytime the state called a witness. You were looking for me," she said as he removed her pants and panties. Tears fell down her face.

"Where was you?"

"On a mission."

"Here you go with that secretive shit."

"I have only one secret."

"And what's that?"

She sighed. "You remember the conversation we had at the hospital when you came out of your coma?"

"Every word of it," he said.

"Remember my unofficial mother?"

"Yup."

"Well, she's the chief of police. Her names Quinetta Antionette Williams."

"What the fuck!?"

"Yes, my mother is a cop. But trust me, I'm no rat. I couldn't be in the courtroom because Train would've put her name in it, and I couldn't allow him to do that."

"So you knew about Train?"

"Not until after y'all got locked up. I tried to tell you the day I came to see you down City Jail, but you didn't want me talking about the case. My mother called me and told me one day I was eating at Sip & Bite. She wanted me to stay away from y'all, but I told her I wouldn't."

"She knew about us?"

"Of course, I told her. She said she seen real love in my eyes, so she didn't try to keep me away from you. She just wanted me to stay away from the trial, so her name wouldn't come up."

"So what comes with being a cop's daughter?"

"A lot. When my name is ran in the computer, it comes up that she's my mother, so the police get off my heels," she said. "Now you know all of me. I have no more secrets. So do you trust me now?"

He looked at her. "You do know that trust is earned, not given, right?" he asked.

She walked her naked self out of the room and came back with a gift bag.

"Trust earned now?" she said, handing him the bag.

He looked inside and saw two guns and a wallet.

"What the fuck is this?"

"A murder weapon. A police issued Glock .40. And the cop's wallet that I just killed."

"You didn't," he said, picking up the wallet. He opened it up and saw Train's face. "Oh shit."

"I followed him from your trial one day. He was moving out of his old house. I caught him tonight trying to get the last of the boxes. I killed him Six to the body, four to the face. You have the murder weapon with my prints on it, Train's gun, and his wallet. You are the only one who knows about this, besides me," she said. "Trust earned?" she asked, holding out her hand.

Instead of shaking her hand, he pulled her in for a long, wet, sensual kiss.

"Oh… (muah) now you… (muah) trust me?"

"I have no choice but to now."

"I love you King Tremaine Davenport."

"I love you Queen Azarah Davenport."

"Davenport?" she questioned.

"Yeah, Davenport. Let's get married," he said, sweeping her up in his arms.

"You ready for that, Mr. Davenport?"

"Yup. You?"

"You have to meet my mother first," she giggled.

"Oh shit," he laughed.

***

Boone Street... (Saturday)

The coming home block party for Toe Taggin' Posse Music Group was in full blast mode. It seemed like the entire city came out to show their love and support.

Jerrod, Nyse, DY, Amil, Trina, Azarah, L-Trigga, 4Hunnid, Madd Lou, Sos'a, Wild Bill, Taedo, Flee, Connie Y, and Magik was all behind the stage that they had set up on the block.

"So who's the best man, 4Hunnid?" Amil asked, looking at Azarah's colorless, princess cut, flawless four carat diamond engagement ring.

"Shit, all my men are my best men. All my niggas gon' be on the front line."

"You better believe it," Magik said.

Dee Dee came back there where they were. "Yo, it's some broad with some big glasses and a big hat on out here talking about she need to see 4Hunnid or Magik."

"Who she say she is?"

"She won't say."

Magik got up and left with Dee Dee. Everyone else continued discussing the wedding.

"Yeah, we decided on the courthouse marriage, and go all out on everything else. My man's not traditional, and neither am I."

"I'm planning the bachelorette party," Trina said, causing everyone to laugh.

Magik walked back to them with a fine light-skin woman behind him with a body like Beyonce, and a butt like Ledisi.

"Look who it is 4Hunnid," Magik said.

He looked, but didn't recognize her. She removed her glasses and hat, and 4Hunnid almost fell out of his chair.

"Get the fuck outta here," he smiled in shock. "Damn, you look good." Azarah looked at him like she wanted to snatch his head off.

"Hey baby," she sung, and walked over to hug him.

All eyes went on her ass; females included.

"Hey everyone. They know me as Jamie. I use to buy drugs from them, once upon a time. I owe my life to these two. I was with Range Rover Rivers the day he was murdered. I changed after that; with the help of these guys and this girl," she said, pointing to Trina.

"Oh shit, Jamie! I took you shopping that time. Damn, you look different, girl."

"Money will do that to you, Trina."

"That's why you all hidden under that hat and those glasses?"

"No. You all have the ever-so-nosy media out there. How would it look if someone snapped a photo of Lisa Jamie Gibson, the wife of Judge Rodger Gibson, at a Toe Taggin' Posse party?"

Everyone's mouths dropped. It took everyone a second to process what she just dropped on them.

"We were going back to trial, wasn't we?" Magik asked.

"Yup. I didn't know the case he was complaining about everyday was y'all, until the day tho lawyers filed the motions to dismiss. He was going to declare a mistrial and have you all pick another jury. But the power of the three Ps is enough in any case."

"Three Ps?" Trina questioned.

"Power. Pussy. Persuasion."

"I know that's right," she said, high fiving Jamie.

"Thanks Jamie. We really appreciate that. If there's anything you—"

"I'm fine Magik. More than fine. Just stay out of trouble for me. I love y'all," she said, putting her glasses and hat back on.

"We love you too," 4Hunnid said.

"Time to get this show on the road gentlemen and ladies," Flee said.

***

Jerrod and L-Trigga went out on the stage and thanked everyone for their support and love for the label, their affiliates, and businesses. After they were done talking they introduced the Toe Taggin' Posse; The Wild Hunnids and Trojan Boyz and the first lady.

Azarah kicked off their set with *I Love My Man*. After she was done, the boyz took over. The beat dropped for their song *TOE TAGGIN' POSSE*

FOREVER. Madd Lou grabbed a mic from Flee and went in. The crowd started screaming his name.

The show, day, and event, went off without any problems, but it was a group of young wolves in the crowd, adding the faces of the Toe Taggin' Posse to their memory banks. There was always someone looking to come up in the concrete jungle. It's a constant struggle to stay on top.

Anyone that's ever been on top will tell you, it's easy to obtain the crown… It's even harder to retain it.

TOE TAGGIN' POSSE

Epilogue

Clearance Mitcholl Jr. Courthouse...
Quinette Antionette Williams placed the hand of her adopted daughter in the hands of the reputed gang member; King Tremaine Davenport. She leaned over to 4Hunnid, so that her lips were almost touching his ear. "Take care of my child with your life. She loves you and I love her, so I have no choice but to like you, but if my baby is harmed by you or about you, I will come after you and the rest of the Toe Tagging Posse, no prosecutors involved." A shiver ran down 4Hunnid's spine. "Love you son-in-law," she said, and kissed his cheek.

The preacher went on with the service. They put the rings on one another.

"Do you, King Tremaine Davenport, take Queen Azarah Williams to be your lawfully wedded wife…"

"I do," he said, looking into her eyes.

"And do you, Queen Azarah Williams, take King Tremaine Davenport to be your lawfully wedded husband…"

"I sure do."

"By the power invested in me, I now pronounce you husband and wife. You may now kiss the bride."

Everyone clapped for the couple.

"I never thought I'd see this day, my nigga," Madd Lou said.

"Shid, I did," L-Trigga said, "sucka for love-ass nigga."

4Hunnid laughed. "I couldn't help it relative. It was the Balenciaga that got me," 4Hunnid said, laughing.

"So, where y'all going for the honeymoon?" Connie Y asked.

"I told him to take me to the Cayman Islands for a week, then to Barbados for a week, a week in Costa Rica, and then end it with a week in Turks and Caicos'. I got it all planned out."

"Okay, big ballers," she said, as they walked out of the room.

"Come on y'all, we got a party to go to," Dee Dee said, grabbing the back of Azarah's long dress.

At this point it wasn't a secret that the Chief of Police's daughter was seeing 4Hunnid, so Quinetta had no problem with being seen with them on certain occasions. She walked out of the courthouse along with everyone else. The talking had stopped once they walked out of the courthouse, causing Quinetta to turn around. Everyone had stood motionless and was looking around like something was off. Their street instincts had kicked in full time.

"FUCK TOE TAGGIN' POSSE!" they all heard someone scream before 4Hunnid was struck with a bullet.

Kak-Kak-Kak-Kak-Kak-Kak-Kak!
Fock! Fock! Fock! Fock! Fock!
Tat- Tat-Tat-Tat-Tat-Tat-Tat!

St. Paul Street sounded like Iraq in war time. The fully automatic weapons seemed to go on forever, and the crazed laughter that accompanied the bullets made it worse.

Magik looked up from the steps of the courthouse, a bloody mess, and saw Looney Redz holding a AR-15, and two dusty looking kids holding AK-47s.

His last thoughts were of the engagement ring he had in his pocket, that he was going to present to Trina at 4Hunnid and Azarah's wedding party. His last words were, "Toe Taggin' Posse, bitch." The shots just kept on coming.

To Be Continued...

OTHER

BOOKS

BY KAYO

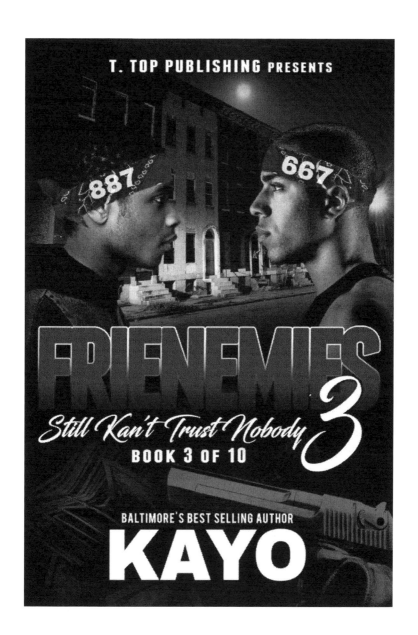

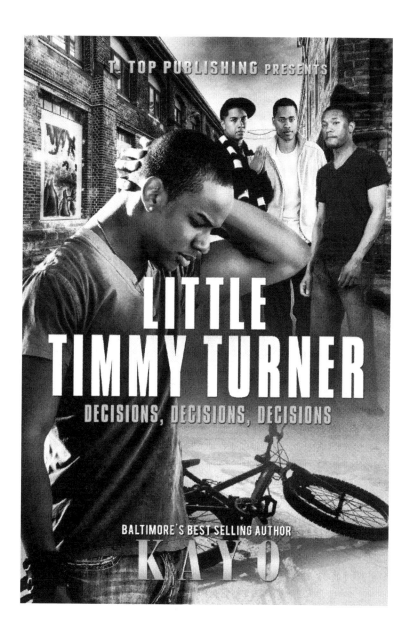

COMING

SOON

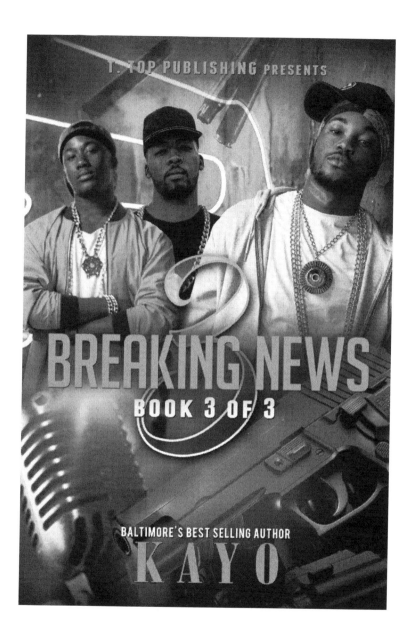

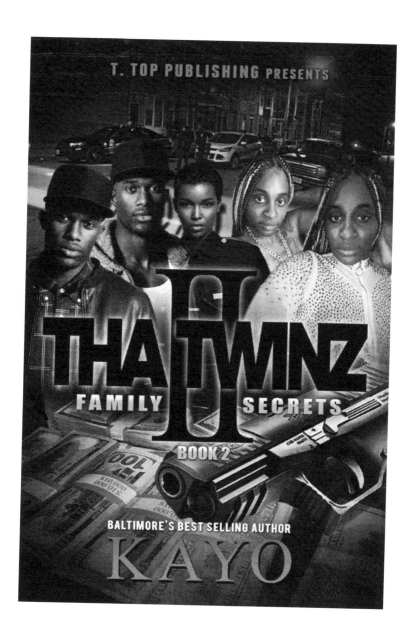

Made in the USA
Columbia, SC
14 March 2022

57666758R00124